GRACIES POND

BY

MARK R. FORTUNE

To Zane,
You are a light in so many people's life.
You will always be a special person to me.
We will always walk this road together.
I love you in so many ways
Your Grand Pa Sponsor
Mark R Fortune

This book is a work of fiction. Places, events, and situations in this story are purely fictional. Any resemblance to actual persons, living or dead, is coincidental.

© 2004 by Mark R. Fortune. All rights reserved.

No part of this book may be reproduced, stored in a retrieval system, or transmitted by any means, electronic, mechanical, photocopying, recording, or otherwise, without written permission from the author.

ISBN: 1-4140-3811-9 (e-book)
ISBN: 1-4140-3809-7 (Paperback)
ISBN: 1-4140-3810-0 (Dust Jacket)

This book is printed on acid free paper.

1stBooks - rev. 12/15/03

Dedication

To my parents, Margaret and Robert,
for giving me the opportunity to learn to read and write.

Table of Contents

Chapter One 1

Chapter Two 7

Chapter Three 14

Chapter Four 21

Chapter Five 28

Chapter Six 31

Chapter Seven 35

Chapter Eight 42

Chapter Nine 48

Chapter Ten 49

Chapter Eleven 53

Chapter Twelve 55

Chapter Thirteen 63

Chapter Fourteen 66

Chapter Fifteen 70

Chapter Sixteen 76

Chapter Seventeen 83

Chapter Eighteen 88

Chapter Nineteen 94

Chapter Twenty 97

Chapter Twenty-One 104

Chapter Twenty-Two 123

Chapter Twenty-Three 131

Chapter Twenty-Four 138

Chapter Twenty-Five 146

Chapter Twenty-Six 152

Chapter Twenty-Seven 162

Chapter Twenty-Eight 167

Chapter Twenty-Nine 176

Chapter Thirty 181

Chapter Thirty-One 196

Chapter Thirty-Two 205

Chapter Thirty-Three 212

Chapter Thirty-Four 220

Chapter Thirty-Five 230

Chapter Thirty-Six 250

Chapter Thirty-Seven 257

About the Author 277

Chapter One

A cold, stiff wind had started blowing late last night. Buck knew then that it was time to get to work. In the light of the moon, he started moving his small amount of stock in to pens, corrals and the barn. The wind was not letting up all night.

As the dawn was breaking in the East, Buck had just taken an armload of wood in to the house and was stoking the fire. Warmth was what he needed now. Changed into a clean pair of jeans and a blue flannel shirt (all he ever wore), Buck sat down at the kitchen window and looked out over his land, savoring his coffee with just a touch of whiskey in it. Lately, that was the only time he drank alcohol. As he was watching the sun coming up in the East, he also noticed the ominous, heavy laden, snow clouds building up over the sand hills to the Northwest.

This was the time of year he disliked the most, too little to do and too much time to think and remember.

As a young boy, his older brother Bill and he couldn't wait until the first snowfall. A lot of the time they couldn't go to school due to the roads being snowed over. So, after morning chores they would sled down Bill's Hill. Named after Bill since he was the first one to ride it from top to bottom all at one try.

We didn't have anyone else to play with, as the closest neighbor was half a mile away. All they had was Gracie, and who needs a girl? Probably couldn't even throw a snowball! Bill and I would be rich if we had a nickel for every snowball we threw. Bill was not just my big brother; he was also my best friend.

The sound of gravel crunching under tires brought Buck out of his daydream. Picking up his cup of coffee, Buck found it had gotten lukewarm. Looking out his window and downing his coffee, he saw Ed Barnes, the county vet, coming up on Buck's property. Turning under the eight by eight structure with the Rocking B's sign above and crossing the cattle guard; dust blowing to the South. "Won't be long before there won't be any dust" Buck thought looking at the clouds getting closer.

Ed pulled up to the wooden plank porch just as Buck had opened the front door. A cold wind that felt like ice met Buck's face. "Come on in" Buck yelled above the wind, as Ed climbed out of his rust bucket he called a truck.

Ed had one hand on his Stetson and his medical bag in the other as he clamored up the three steps to the porch and stepped quickly across the porch and through the storm door. Closing it quickly and then the wooden door behind it. "How ya been, Buck?" asked Ed. "Getting along just fine Ed, coffee?"

Buck asked. "Can't stay long, just left the Nelson's place down the road, figured I'd drop in since I was so close. Storm coming up and all, just thought I'd check on you. Animals alright?"

"Yep, got' em all in last night" Buck said as he poured two cups of coffee. "Let's sit here at the table for a bit" Buck said.

Ed removed his Stetson and Sheepskin coat, hanging them on the hat rack by the door asked "Heard from Bill Lately?"

"Got a letter from him the other day, wasn't much to it. Telling me about how much he hates the city, crime and all. Says he can't make the money he's making here that he's making there. Says him and boy are just fine", Buck answered.

Buck and Ed just sat with hands around their cups, looking out the window.

Shame about Bill losing Emily the way he did", Ed said. "Wouldn't have lost his wife if he wasn't so all fired up about living in that city and making that big money", Buck said angrily.

"You thought a lot of Emily, didn't you? Ed said. "She was a good woman Ed, ain't many of those around. She liked it out here. I wish Bill would have moved here before the accident. Not that much traffic out here. Damn drunk drivers!"

Ed noticed a slight tear well up in Buck's eye.

"Well Buck, wish I could stay longer", Ed said finishing off his coffee. "Where's Turk by the way?" Turk was Buck's 3-year-old Labrador. "That black devil's out chasing phantom rabbits or down at the pond getting in a swim before the storm", Buck said.

"Speaking of storms, I better get going", Ed said. Getting back into his jacket and hat, the sound of scratching came at the door. "There's Turk now, guess he's had enough" Buck said. They both chuckled at this.

Turk bolted through the door as it was opened, stopped, sniffed Ed's pants then sat down, begging. Ed closed the door still inside and produced a piece of beef jerky from his pocket. Turk's ears perked up and he cocked his head to the left, licked his muzzle and sat patiently looking at his doctor-friend. Turk raised his right paw and Ed gave him the treat. Turk then retreated to the throw rug in front of the fireplace and commenced to consume his reward.

"You spoil that dog, Ed" Buck said. "And you don't?" Ed replied with a smile.

Ed shook Buck's hand, said "See ya later" and was out the door.

The wind had let down a little, Ed waved as he made a circle in front of the house and headed toward the gate. Dust billowing up behind him as he headed east toward town.

Buck stood at the window watching until Ed and the dust trail were out of sight. Buck sat back at the table looking at the road and his mind wandered back.

A cloud of dust coming hell bent for leather, proceeded by a red '52 Chevy pickup, was coming towards the gate. Both Bill and I knew that there was going to be hell to pay within a few minutes. Driving that truck was our Dad and sitting next to him was a screaming, perplexed and irate woman, our Mom.

Mom and Dad (others knew them as Maggie and Bob Stevens) went into town every other weekend for groceries and such and Mom would tell Dad how to drive all the way. When Bill and I weren't with them the same thing happened every time.

Dad would wait until he was about one mile form our place and he would drive like the Devil was after him, all the way to our gate, slide through the gate and cruise to the porch, everything learned to stay out of the way.

When stopped at the porch, Mom would smack Dad on the back of his head with her open hand and Dad would just laugh. Mom would say "Bob Stevens you are some kind of fool" then she would get out of the truck and Dad would continue to laugh, all though not quite as robustly.

Mom would stomp across the porch, go in the house, firmly close the front door and go to her room, Thus leaving the three of us to carry the boxes of groceries in. After the groceries were put up Mom would come out and tell Dad "you nearly scared the dickens out of me", and Dad with a little smile would say" I just don't know what got into me, Honey. Then they would kiss each other. Then Dad would wink at Bill and me.

A nudge from a cold nose brought Buck back to today. Turk was sitting beside him with his big yellow eyes saying "lunchtime." "Okay boy" Buck said rising from his chair. "Let's see what we have." With Turk by his side, bacon and beans were fixed for lunch, both of their favorite.

As predicted, snowflakes as large as nickels began to fall outside.

Chapter Two

The alarm said 6:00 AM. and Bill reached sleepily across and turned it off. Sitting on the side of the bed, Bill stretched and felt all thirty-nine years of bumps and bruises. Rising, Bill walked into the hallway, knocked on BJ's door, "Time to get up and at em" Bill said.

Bill Jr., better known as BJ, barely coming out of his coma sighed "Okay Dad." Bill continued down the hall, and turned into the bathroom. After relieving himself, Bill washed his hands and face. Toweling himself dry, Bill leaned over and picked up the silver framed 8x10 picture of his wife and kissed it. I love you, Honey" and like every morning a lump grew in his throat. Leaving the bathroom, and what seemed like every morning for the last twelve years, came back to BJ's door, knocked and heard an immediate and slightly defiant "I'm up Dad."

Bill, being a single parent for the last six months, had removed himself from everything except his son and work.

Since Emily's accident took her out of his world, Bill didn't have any zest for life. Everything seemed so useless.

Work was the easiest as it kept his mind busy and full. Driving to and from work and at night were the hardest. Too many memories, passing stores they shopped at or restaurants Emily and him had eaten at seemed to draw his attention, and pain and loss would fill his heart.

Passing the park on Clay Road, and looking at the teeter totter, Bill would see Emily holding BJ on one end and himself on the other end laughing and squealing as up and down they went. So many years...So many memories.

Bill was dropping the second scoop of coffee grinds into to the paper filter when he heard BJ's door open. "Mornin' Dad", BJ said in a voice that was still in the process of changing from that of a boy to that of a man.

"Good morning Son, sleep well?" Bill asked, turning from the coffee maker to his son.

"All right I guess" BJ replied as he reached for a glass from the cupboard. As Bill watched his son cross the kitchen towards the fridge, he noticed how much like his mother he was, with his red hair and small frame, which he had no way of concealing since all he had on was his briefs. No reason for modesty since it was just the two of them. BJ poured himself a glass of orange juice, and closing the door asked, "How about you Dad, get any sleep?"

BJ knew the answer, it was always the same "Like a rock" but he could see it in Dad's eyes and posture. Dad had lost a lot of weight and his shoulders kind of slumped down and forward, his head seeming like it was too heavy to hold up, seemed to always be hanging down, and grayish bags were under his slightly bloodshot eyes.

"Like a rock, Son!" Bill answered quietly.

BJ retreated to his room to get dressed for school. On the closing of the door, Bill sitting at the table, put his head in his hands and closed his watering eyes. Bill had no one to talk to about how he felt. Thoughts of suicide came and went. Only the love for his son kept him from carrying out such an act, when the depression and remorse got so deep at times. Those that he did talk to, mostly co-workers, would say: "You'll get through this, It takes time, It will get better." How the hell did they know! None of them had their whole life mangled in a car by some DRUNKEN SON-OF-A-BITCH.

Paul Webb who worked at the next drafting table, who was much older than Bill, had given him the best advice. Paul had said, I have a philosophy about life Bill, It's one day at a time, we can handle anything, one day at a time", and he said no more about it.

Bill raised his face from his hands at the sound of BJ's door opening and heard BJ close the bathroom door. Bill was very glad his son had not come into the kitchen and caught his dad crying. Bill walked to the sink, ran cold water into his cupped hands and splashed water in his face a number of times and toweled it dry with a dish towel hanging on the rack. He went to the mug rack on the counter, pulled a coffee mug off and turning to the coffee maker, realized he hadn't turned it on.

Too late for that now, he thought. More time had passed than he allowed for his morning routine. He carried his mug to the fridge, found the orange juice and poured himself half a cup, all that was left, closed the fridge and tossed the empty carton into the trash.

BJ came out of the bathroom dressed for school with his Houston Rockets ball cap and sweatshirt on above his dungarees and Nike tennis shoes. He said, "Dad, I need my lunch money" noticing Dad still in his pajama bottoms added, "Are you alright?"

"Yes son, just running a little late!" Bill went into his room and came out handing BJ two dollars said "Now, get going or you'll miss your bus!"

BJ gave his dad a hug and said "I love you Dad." "I love you to" Bill said. Then BJ was out the front door, into the humid and slightly cool Houston air.

Bill also running late, hurried into his room, threw on his pants, dress shirt, socks and shoes, slung his tie around his neck, went into the bathroom, brushed his hair and teeth, grabbed his portable electric razor, through the house to the hall closet, grabbed his windbreaker and hurried through the front door. Turing to lock the door "Damn, where are my keys?"

Bill exclaimed. Rushing back into the house and to his room, Bill found that not only had he forgotten his keys, but also his wallet, change and belt! Everything that was in or on his pants from yesterday.

Finally locking the door behind him. Bill walked to his black BMW in the garage, hitting his alarm and hearing the familiar beep-beep as the car unlocked. Bill realized he had better slow down or he would end up in a wreck.

Luckier than most people in Houston, he only had a short way to work, about twenty-five to thirty minutes depending on traffic.

Bill drove at a reasonably sane pace while he shaved but got into a faster pace when he heard the radio announcer say, "If you have to be at work at eight, you have ten minutes."

Bill arrived at work at two minutes after eight and was already tired. Walking rapidly up the walkway and fixing his tie as he passed through the automatic sliding doors of GM&T Architectural Designs Inc., he thought, "Thank God it's Friday."

Paul was sitting by his drafting table when Bill came into their office holding a cup of coffee in his hand.

"Good morning Bill, saw you coming up the walk and figured I'd pour you a cup too", Paul said pointing at a cup sitting by Bill's table.

"Thanks Paul and good morning to you too", Bill said. Paul like BJ, had noticed how Bill had not seemed to be getting any better since Emily's death, decided it was time to see if he could help Bill. Normally Paul was the type of man to stay out of people's business unless someone asked for help. Once asked, he would give his all, sharing his strength, hope, and experience. At fifty-two years old he had plenty, and that was all he had to offer.

"Bill, I was wondering, since we have a pretty light work-load today."

Bill's mind shot forward thinking, "No, don't say we are going home early."

"I was wondering if maybe you and I could go out and have an extra long lunch today." Paul finished.

"Well, I don't think I should lea..." Bill started.

"Bill, in the two plus years we have been working together we have never had lunch together, outside of this office that is! Come on it will be my treat.

Bill hesitated slightly, then said, "Okay, what the hell, be good to get away from here for a while!"

In Bill's hesitation Paul noticed something he had known so well, for so long himself, a deep and overpowering fear.

Paul finishing his coffee said, "Good then we have a date, shall I pick you up at twelve?" and they both laughed at this. Paul turned to his table and going through his Rolodex found the number he wanted and dialed the number.

Bill just looked out the window at the gray Houston sky and thought, "That's the first time I have laughed in a long time." It felt good and just the smallest of a smile line deepened on either side of Bill's thin lips.

Chapter Three

Buck and Turk had both finished their lunch, Buck at a pace reserved for people with nowhere to go, and Turk the pace of a vacuum cleaner.

Turk lay asleep on the rug in front of the fireplace, his front paws jerking in rapid, spasmodic movements. Dreaming as dogs do. Buck sitting in his easy chair, watching the flickering fire, went back to a sunnier time.

"Hey Bobby! (Buck's given name), go ask Dad if we can go swimming", Bill said.

"You know we have to have all our chores done", Bobby answered. "I do! Need some help?" Bill asked. A large smile crossed Bobby's face as he yelped, "Sure, just need to finish painting this part of the chicken coop!"

At ten and twelve years old, painting can be a messy job, but Bill and Bobby had a knack, and a good teacher in their father, and were able to do the job neatly.

Pulling together they finished within half an hour, and stood back, with one arm around the others back, with raised brushes in their other hands, and said in unison. "Another job well done by the Stevens brothers." Laughing, they cleaned up and both ran to find their dad.

Being allowed to go swim after Dad's inspection of the coop and a pat on the back was a great reward.

Bill had been reading <u>Treasure Island</u> and so down at the pond we were no longer kids, we were good guys and pirates. Using tomato stakes for swords and hats made of newspaper we sailed the seven seas.

Using a 2x12 board, five feet long, which we had pushed out into the pond, we had an enemy ship to sink. Our cannon balls were dirt clods. We sank many a ship that day.

During such a battle a pickup truck came pulling through our front gate and Bill and I both crouched down to avoid being seen by our make believe enemy. After it passed by the pond/ocean, we resumed our sinking of the enemy ship, not caring much about the visitor.

Immersed in our battle we didn't notice another enemy had approached us from the rear until we heard, "What are you boys doing?" It was Gracie, the Parker's daughter. They must have come by to visit Mom and Dad.

Bill promptly replied, "Boys...we're pirates. I'm the captain and he's my first mate and you're the enemy, so if you don't want to walk the plank, you better shove off!"

"What's that supposed to mean?" Gracie asked "That's pirate talk for you to go back to the house!" Bill said in a commanding voice.

I looked at Captain Bill with a smile on my face and with great admiration. Then, she said, "I don't have to, your folks told me to tell you both to let me play with you!"

The gloom and despair that fell over me was insurmountable. My world had come to an end. If Mom and Dad said it, we had to do it.

"Our parents said we have to let you play with us?" Bill screamed. Gracie, standing on the top of the bank, with her hands on her hips and ponytail going up and down as she nodded said, "That's right." It made me feel like turning inside out. I looked at Bill and couldn't believe my eyes. He was smiling. Then, he winked at me. I was confused.

"Okay," Bill said, but to be a pirate you have to pass an initiation. You have to swim across the pond or you have to leave for good.

My hero had come through again. No one had ever swum across the pond, at least not Bill and I, and she didn't even have a swimsuit on. I knew we had won!

Gracie's blue eyes shifted from us to the pond, surveying the one hundred-fifty foot across, and then walked down the bank toward us. "Okay", she said.

Both of our mouths dropped open at the same time. Gracie sat down at the edge of the water and started taking off her tennis shoes. Bill whispered, "Don't worry she won't go through with it."

"Remember the time we told Peewee Harris to join our club house he had to eat a worm and he did, and we didn't even have a clubhouse", I said.

"Oh yeah I forgot about that", Bill answered.

Standing by the water in her cut off blue jeans and pink blouse, void of shoes and socks, Gracie put one foot ankle deep in the water. "Feels cool", she said with a slight shake in her voice.

"Do you even know how to swim?" Bill asked.

"I've been taking lessons at the Y.M.C.A.", she replied snottily.

Oh how I despised girls, but something about Gracie was beginning to change that in me. I guess it was because she sat down in the dirt and actually got dirt on her. Then, Gracie was up to her knees, then thighs, then waist. Looking back over her left shoulder as if asking "far enough." I noticed a slight shiver run through her. She was already further out than we thought she would go. Seeing that we were not going to tell her that was far enough, she turned and leaned forward and started swimming out toward the middle.

Bill and I looked at each other with surprised and scared expressions on our faces.

Standing there on the bank for what seemed like a lifetime, but actually a matter of seconds, we saw that Gracie could have used more lessons at the "Y". She wasn't swimming like anyone I had ever seen. Of course the only one I had seen was "Tarzan" at the Roxy in town.

Gracie was slapping the water with her hands and making large splashes with her feet. She was getting farther out, and closer to what I feared most, the middle.

We both started hollering as loud as we could at Gracie. "Stop. Come back. That's far enough. Okay, you're a pirate." But, Gracie couldn't hear us. She had her face and ears in the water most of the time.

All of a sudden bill grabbed the old inner tube we used to paddle around in, and ran and jumped in the water and got his butt in the middle and started rowing with his arms out after Gracie.

Then Gracie started losing her rhythm and slowed down and started sinking a little. Bill started rowing faster, his arms looking like paddle wheels.

By now Gracie had made it a little past the middle, kind of like the point of no return.

Then Gracie stopped and started a kind of splashing and disappeared. Bill was steady paddling, but not moving as fast as he had been.

Seeing all of this unfold, I started thinking, "Were going to prison for murder...maybe the electric chair, or gas chamber" I then started screaming, "Oh God...Please God help her, don't' let her die", possibly my first prayer.

Then a hand, her hand, came above the water, then the other hand, and then her head. She was holding onto our enemy ship. The 2x12 had floated out unnoticed by any of us during our confrontation with Gracie.

Bill was very close to Gracie now and I started running around the pond along the well-worn path as fast as my ten-year-old legs could carry me, casting glances toward the pair of them as I went. There seemed to be no sound and everything was in slow motion. Only the beating of my heart. Small limbs slapping at my face and chest went unnoticed. Suddenly, I realized I was directly across from the other side.

Then I heard Bill say, "No you don't have to." Then Gracie pushed the board away and slowly started swimming toward me. I couldn't believe it!

With Bill paddling close behind her at about thirty feet from shore, I started jumping up and down and making outrageous swimming motions with my arms. Coaching Gracie I screamed, "You can make it. Keep going champ." I was still screaming as she came closer and closer. Then, Gracie stopped and so did my heart. When she just stood there waist deep in the pond, I fell flat on my butt, exhausted. Gracie waked up on the shore and plopped down beside me followed by Bill who sat beside her.

Bill looked back and forth at both of us and exclaimed, "The pond has a name, Gracie's Pond."

Waking from his dream Buck opened his eyes. The fire had nearly died out and the light of day was fading. Rising from the easy chair, Buck stoked the fire and added another log as embers rose with the heat and a flame appeared, he smiled. Walking to the front window, in the light left of the day, Buck looked out at Gracie's Pond and then out past the front gate. He could faintly make out a light in a window at Gracie's house.

Chapter Four

Paul and Bill pulled up in the parking lot of "Blues Bar-B-Q." Getting out of his car and looking over to where Bill had parked, Paul noticed Bill was just sitting behind the wheel staring straight out with the car still running. Walking around the front of his car and over to Bill's, Paul leaned over by the window and asked, "We going in or are you going to stare the place down?" Snapping out of his trance, Bill answered, "I don't think I can go in there. It was one of…"

"I know," Paul interrupted, "it was one of yours and Emily's favorite places. It was also one of Debbie and mine too!"

"Debbie, who's Debbie?" Bill asked.

"That's why I chose this place, to tell you about Debbie, and the Bar-B-Q is the best. Now come on in. It will do you good," Paul gently commanded.

Reluctantly Bill turned off the Beamer and climbed out of his car. Taking a few steps away, hit his automatic alarm, thus locking the car.

Stopping in mid-step with Paul by his side, Bill said, "It's been a long time. I just don't know!"

Paul knowing Bill's pain and fear said, "Bill, please walk through this with me. You will be better for it."

Bill with a slight stammer in his voice replied, "I'll try, but we are not sitting at Emily's and my table. Okay?"

As they walked through the door, Paul went first followed by Bill. Paul stopped by the hostess stand and read the sign, "Please seat yourself, hostess not on duty." Being the slow time of the day, this was appropriate. Inside there were approximately twenty small tables with red and white checkered table cloths and four wooden high backed chairs with cushions matching the table cloths tied to the backs of the chairs.

As Paul read the sign, bill walked past him as if in a trance. Bill's only focus was on a table in the corner. It seemed to pull him as if it were a magnet and he was "the tin man."

Paul stood and watched as Bill stopped at the table, his left hand settled so lightly on the back of a chair, and his right hand went again to his heart. Paul knew this pain.

Walking up behind Bill, Paul put his hand on Bill's shoulder and said, "It's alright." Paul left Bill's side and walked around the table and pulled out the chair.

Bill's eyes riveted to the chair to his left hadn't noticed Paul until he said, "Are we going to sit or stand here all day?" With a slight jerk of his head, eyes training Paul, Bill came back to the present.

"This was our table. I can't sit here!", Bill said. "It's what you need to do Bill. Please sit down."

With some hesitation, Bill pulled his chair out and sat down, resting both hands palm down on the table. His left hand, as if it had a mind of its own, glided a few inches across the table cloth towards the chair to his left. His eyes followed his hand.

In a choked whisper Bill said, "She always sat to my left. Did you know that and why?"

Paul responded, "No. Why?" Knowing Bill didn't hear but needed to tell him. Paul knew the power of this therapy.

Bill continued oblivious to Paul's answer, "Emily was left handed and, of course, I am right handed. She sat to my left so we could hold hands and still eat or drink."

Paul could see the tears welling up in Bill's eyes, and seeing the waitress approaching the table, waved her off. Looking back at Bill and following Bill's gaze, Paul saw Bill's hand turn palm up and finger slightly curl up as if he was holding a hand.

"Bill...Bill!" Paul said.

With a jerk of his head towards Paul, Bill said, "What?"

"I would like to tell you a little story," Paul said, and then continued.

"I had a friend once who had a lovely wife and two beautiful daughters. One Sunday afternoon after drinking a six pack or so, my friend became bored sitting around the house, so he decided that he was going to take his family on a Sunday drive. You with me Bill?" Paul asked.

"Yeah, yeah. What's this all about?", Bill asked.

About this time the waitress came up again, so Bill and Paul ordered the special with tea.

Paul continued when she left. "The girls being thirteen and fifteen years old were in their room on the phone, or listening to their radios, or whatever, and his wife was sewing. My friend asked them all to go with him for a drive. They all declined his request as they were content with what they were doing. My friend became angry that they would not comply with his request, so he made it an order to all three of them. "They were going whether they liked it or not, and right now!" His wife, trying to spare their daughters, said she would go, but the girls could stay home. My friend's plans for a family drive would have none of that, and he demanded that they all go!

They were interrupted by the waitress as she arrived with their order. Being the house special, it was always served quickly. Paul took a drink of his tea as Bill thanked the waitress and Paul continued. "After a few hours of driving and a few more beers, my friend became lost on his trip through the country just north of here.

His wife and daughters, knowing how my friend got when he was drinking, became very quiet.

When my friend made another wrong turn his wife told him so, and that he needed to stop for directions. Well, this made my friend go off into a rage, and looking at his wife told her to "Shut her mouth." Bill noticed a crack in Paul's voice. Paul took another sip of tea and continued.

"That's the last thing my friend remembers. Two weeks later my friend came to in a hospital. They buried Debbie, Stacy, and Stephanie during that time...my wife and my daughters!"

Bill sat back abruptly in his chair as if pushed by some invisible hand. "My God!", Bill said.

"For the next eight years guilt ruled my life, and I let know one know it. I cursed God every day and asked him why. I stayed as drunk as I could get. Always running away from the truth. Of course I lost my job. I slept in cardboard boxes in the wintertime and under bridges most of the time. Eating very rarely, and then it was what I could find in dumpsters behind restaurants. For all those years I couldn't accept that I couldn't bring them back or change that it happened!" Paul said.

"But look at you now! What happened?", Bill asked.

Paul continued, "I apparently overdosed on some grain alcohol, and would up in a state hospital in Utica, New York. Didn't even know what city I was in, or much more, what state, or how I got from Houston to there. Long story short, I ended up in Alcoholics Anonymous. Best thing that ever happened to me! I came to believe in God again, and that I can never change the past. You see, Bill, the past is like a bullet. Once fired you can never bring it back, kind of like the spoken word. Once you have said it, you can't change it."

"Yeah, I see what you mean," Bill said.

"What I'm getting at Bill, is I have been watching you for the last six months since Emily's accident. I felt your pain, but now it is time for you to get on with your life. Sure you're going to miss her and love her, just as I do my family, every time one of their birthdays comes around, or when our anniversary date comes up. But it gets easier with time. Yours hasn't, Bill!"

"I told you my story so you can see you're not alone anymore. Your not the only one this kind of thing has happened to. You're lucky Bill, you still have your son and he probably needs you more than you know," Paul said.

"You're right, Paul, I have been so wrapped up in my own misery that I have forgotten about BJ. I guess I just figured he was okay," Bill said.

He has probably been talking to someone, a friend or teacher, or maybe even a counselor. They do that these days! But he still needs you the most!", Paul said.

They sat in silence through most of their dinner. Bill kept going over in his mind what Paul had said about the past being gone forever. Paul knew that Bill was deciphering what he had told him, and knowing that by telling someone else one more time about his tragedy, he had also helped himself. They were comfortable in the silence.

As Bill and Paul left the cafe, Paul asked, "You okay Bill?"

"Yeah, I feel like I just...I don't know exactly how to describe it," Bill said.

"Like something is a little looser around your throat and that you are walking a little lighter?" Paul asked.

"Yeah, yeah, something like that," Bill said with a smile.

"Go home and enjoy your weekend with your son, Bill. I'll finish up at the office," Paul said.

"I think I will do just that, Paul," Bill said.

As Paul turned away Bill called out to him, "Paul."

Paul turning back said, "What?"

"Thank you," Bill said.

Paul smiled and said, "Have a good day, Bill. It's the only one we have."

Chapter Five

As BJ climbed off the school bus, walking next to his best friend, Chipper, they were planning what they were going to do this weekend as it was Friday. All of a sudden BJ stopped dead in his tracks. Chipper had taken another step when he turned and saw a look on BJ's face that startled him.

"What's the matter, dude?" asked Chipper.

"Look!" said BJ, pointing past Chipper's shoulder.

"What?" said Chipper looking in the direction BJ was pointing. "My dad's car, it is in the driveway. Something must be wrong!" BJ replied. "Maybe he just came home early. His job is his life since Mom died. The last time he was home before me was when he was there to tell me about Mom's accident."

"Well come on, man. We can't stand here all day. I'll walk with you…I will be right by your side," Chipper said.

"You always have been…you always have been," BJ said.

As the pair walked the rest of the way up the street in silence, Chipper put his arm around BJ's shoulder, and he could feel his best friend shivering. Chipper said a short prayer to himself, "God, let it be okay," and both their guardian angels smiled.

As the pair reached the front porch, BJ reached into his pocket and withdrew his door key, his hand shaking so badly he couldn't get the key in the lock. "Oh man," Chipper reached over and took the key gently from his friend's hand and opened the lock for him. "Thanks, man," BJ said and grasped the door handle and opened the door. A sound came from inside the house that was puzzling, yet familiar.

"What's that sound?" asked Chipper.

BJ kind of cocked his head to the side and, looking at Chipper, started to smile.

"Man...that's 'Comet Avenger'. My dad's favorite video game!" BJ said. With a slap on the shoulder BJ replied, "Thanks for coming in with me, but everything is cool. I'll call you later. Maybe you can come and spend the night!" Chipper stood there for a second, and then shrugged his shoulders. "Sounds cool, man," and Chipper turned and headed out the door.

BJ closed the door and started walking toward the sound. As he came close to his room, he stopped at his door and looked in. He saw his dad playing the video game, oblivious to all around him.

As BJ stood there looking in at his father, he saw himself and his dad sitting side-by-side playing. Sometimes they played against each other, and sometimes as partners against some evil villain. Then he heard his mother's voice, "Hey you guys, supper is ready." With a smile on his lips and a tear welling up in his eyes, BJ entered his room.

Wiping his sleeve across his eyes, BJ said, "What's up Dad?"

Bill kind of jumped a little at the sound of his son's voice. "Just thought I would see if I could still fly this star fighter," Bill responded with a big smile on his face. A bigger smile came across BJ's face as he said, "It's like riding a bicycle, Dad."

"I need a partner to win this battle. Care to help out your old dad?" Bill asked.

"It would be my honor, Captain," BJ said and laughed.

Then BJ said to himself, "Thank you God for bringing my dad back." They played through the afternoon and then stopped for supper, both wishing they could hear that familiar voice down the hall.

At the supper table they talked about how they were feeling, and the healing began.

Chapter Six

The weekend passed and the healing had definitely begun. Bill had called Paul a couple of times, one to thank him for being there when he needed a friend, and the second time because he found himself drifting back under that dark cloud of depression and remorse. Paul had told him, "What you are experiencing now, Bill, is normal, and it will come back time and again, but each time it comes back, Bill…it will be to a lesser degree. The main thing you have to do now is accept that you can't change a thing that has happened in the past. The past is like a bullet, once fired it's finished. That bullet will never come back to the cartridge again. It's like the spoken word. Once you have said it, you can't take it back no matter how hard you try."

Bill had very few friends these days. Unlike most married couples, Bill and Emily had been very content with spending the majority of their time with each other. That being neither good nor bad, it did leave a large void in Bill's life. Now it was time to start having a life with his son. Hell, it was time to start having a life for him!

Bill was standing in the kitchen cooking some French fries when he heard the front door open. "I was just about to call over to Chipper's to let you know it was time to come home. It is a school night you know!" exclaimed Bill. "Sorry Dad, just kind of got caught up in a movie we were watching," said BJ, as he reached into the bowl of fries his father had cooked.

"If you are hungry, son, I can cook you up something," Bill said.

"No, I ate over at chippers. I just can't pass up at least tasting a couple of your homemade fries," BJ said as he grabbed a small handful and headed toward his room.

"Hey, you want to watch television or something later on?" Bill asked after him.

"Not right now, I have some geography to study. We are studying about Nebraska right now. Maybe they will say something about Grampa's area. That would be cool, huh?" BJ said, as he closed his bedroom door.

Bill stood there with the saltshaker in his hand thinking about how Emily used to get on him about using too much salt, and once more he was amazed at how much she was a part of his life. Everywhere he turned, she was there…still.

About that time BJ came bursting out of his room, "Dad, I think this might be around Grampa's place!"

"Well, let me see what you found," said Bill.

"See, right here, Dad, their talking about the sand hills region of Nebraska near Kearny. Isn't that where you went to college?" asked BJ.

"Well yes, it was where I went to college for my first year, but that is a good hundred miles from where your grandpa lives, or should I say where your Uncle Bob lives," answered Bill.

"Well, when you think about the size of the entire world, a hundred miles isn't that much is it?" proclaimed BJ.

"No, not when you put it in that context, Son. I guess it's not that far," answered Bill with a chuckle.

As BJ walked back to his room, Bill heard him say, "Well, I think it's cool."

Bill sat down at the kitchen table and started to realize how much he had missed BJ and how much of his life had been consumed with the loss of Emily. He remembered reading somewhere before Emily's death that grief had to run it's course, and it took different lengths of time for everyone. Six months had passed and he could barely remember anything but the funeral. Staring out at the fading light of the day, Bill remembered something else he hadn't thought of in a long time, his little brother.

He did remember that when he called up to Gracie's (Bob had the phone disconnected when he took over the ranch) to tell her of Emily's death, and to get in touch with Bob, he was nowhere to be found. Gracie started her condolences and said he was off on another one of his benders. They both agreed that Bob bad never been the same since he came back from Viet Nam.

Unfortunately, Bob missed the funeral and called a week or so later, drunk of course, and started cussing Bill for making his work and the almighty dollar more important than his family's safety. He said that it was Bill's fault that Emily had been killed. Bill slammed the phone down and had not spoken to Bob since.

Bill said out loud, "My God, that's been six months since that happened! I am going to give Gracie a call tonight!"

Chapter Seven

As Bill was thinking about his little brother, his little brother's mind was not on Bill. As Buck stood there looking out into the darkness at the faint light coming across the distance from Gracie's windows, he couldn't help but wander back over the years. They had known each other since that day on the pond. Later, Bill and he had both learned how to swim there with Gracie's tutoring. On through the years, Bob's admiration for Gracie had never faltered.

Bob, being a year older and a grade ahead of her in school, starting noticing his feelings change for her somewhere in his senior year to those of more than a friend. Gracie had changed, what seemed like, right before his eyes, literally.

He had been in a hurry to get to class and rounding a corner had run smack into Gracie knocking books and papers out of both of their hands and all over the place. While helping each other pick them up, amid numerous apologies, their eyes met and a feeling he had never felt for Gracie, coursed through his entire body. He jumped back, apologizing again for running into her. Also in a flutter, she was saying it was okay, and then Bob hurried away not daring to look back in case she saw the flushed look on his face. If he had, he would have seen the same look on hers.

Bob couldn't figure out what these feelings were, and with Bill gone off to college, he had no one to talk to. He had friends, but Bob didn't think this was something you mentioned to them, and definitely not to Dad. That would only end up either in, "I don't have time right now," or "go ask your mom." So, he did finally ask Mom and she just smiled and said, "Oh, you will figure it out someday." She then gave him a hug and went on about her cleaning.

Being basically shy, he never asked her out on a date. After all, they were best friends, but lately he felt more than a friend. He had a yearning deep down inside him to…Hell he didn't know what it was except total confusion.

As time went by Bob graduated and within two weeks had enlisted in the Marines. The draft was in full effect at this time and by 1967, if you were healthy, middle class to poor, and not in college or married by the time you were eighteen, you were bound for the Service and Viet Nam.

Gracie came to the bus station with his mom and dad to see him off. She wore a yellow summer dress that really highlighted her womanly features (a vision he carried through many night there after). She kissed him goodbye a little longer than a friendship kiss should have lasted. That was when he knew...he loved her.

In boot camp, he had written her more than he had his mom and dad. Never, letting her know his true feelings. In their letters Bob had mentioned how the other guys in his company would tease him about not having a girlfriend, so Gracie had sent him a picture of her and told him to tell them that she was his girlfriend.

Home on leave, before shipping out to Viet Nam, Bob had finally asked Gracie out on a real date. To his surprise, Gracie was very excited about going out with him. In fact, her answer was, "I thought this day would never come." The two of them were inseparable during the month he was home. Gracie's senior year had just started, so they had to be satisfied with whatever time they could be together. Bob didn't talk much about Viet Nam, but he did talk about the training he had been through, and that alone scared Gracie.

Bob wore his uniform, mostly at his mom's request, anytime they went to church or to visit anyone. Bob was also very proud of his uniform, with its expert rifleman and Viet Nam campaign ribbon over the left pocket and the one stripe on the sleeves. Full of gung-ho and John Wayne ideology, he was going to win the war single handedly. That would change in more ways than one.

There had been some pretty heavy making out between the two of them the month he was home. Trying to make up for lost time. The last night before he was to fly back to San Diego, Gracie had suggested they just go for a drive for a little while. They ended up on Skull Hill (named after a skull that was found belonging to a man that had been buried there back in the old wagon train days), and that night, between two hearts, a memory they would carry their entire lives was given birth to. Gracie had told Bob how for so many years she had loved him, and Bob had told her about the way his feelings had been changing for her also, and then he told her that he loved her. They sat wrapped in each others arms on the tailgate of that old truck for what seemed like hours, watching the full moon rise over the hills to the east, their hearts melded into one.

Bob and Gracie arrived back at Gracie's house a little before 5:00 P.M. and they kissed goodbye, as Bob had to be home for a special dinner his mom was having for his last night home.

Driving through the front gate Bob spotted Bill's car parked in front of the house and thought to himself, "I hope he doesn't start all that shit about making love, not war."

The night went well, and with a call to Gracie to tell her he loved her again and goodnight, Bob slept one of his last peaceful and undisturbed nights.

The next morning found Bill and Bob out on the front porch saying their goodbyes. Bill, being against the war, said he wasn't going to the airport. Bob climbed into the pickup truck with his dad, and Gracie and his mom followed in Gracie's car as there wasn't enough room in the truck and Dad had insisted on driving Bob to Omaha, which was for the best because it gave Bob and his dad time to talk. Being a farmer and rancher never allowed them much time to talk on a one-on-one basis. That trip was monumental in Bob's memories because there were very few times in his life where it was just he and his dad for longer than ten minutes.

Buck was brought back to the present when he heard a whining noise and turned to see Turk lying on his rug with his head between his paws. When Turk saw buck look at him, he came up on all fours like he was spring loaded and, moving toward the door, Turk started rapidly wagging his tail. His whole body was wagging with anticipation in rhythm with his tail.

"Well, where do you think you're going?...guess we should go check the stock and make sure everything's secure for the night," said Buck.

Buck glanced back out the window at the light coming from Gracie's house and then back at Turk. "Maybe we'll go see Gracie for a little bit. Would you like that?"

Turk barked loudly and turned a couple of circles by the door. "Okay, okay, let me get dressed and we will go out together. No sense in letting out more heat than we have to!" Buck said.

Stepping out of the door was quite an awakening. Buck could almost feel his face flush in the cold crisp of the air. "Damn, that will take the wind out of your sails," said Buck. Turk ran through one of the barn doors that was slightly open. "I don't remember leaving that open. It must have been the wind," Buck was thinking aloud.

About this time Buck heard Turk barking and raising all kinds of hell inside the barn. Then he heard another noise he knew way to well. Buck turned, running back to the house, taking two steps at a time up the front steps, crossed the front porch and crashed through the front door. He grabbed his rifle off the rack and cocked it as he turned back out the door crossing the porch at a full run. But, by the sounds he was too late.

Turk had already entered into deadly combat with the scourge of the plains - a coyote. Running toward the barn as fast as his legs would carry him through the foot of snow that was on the ground, Buck could hear the growling and yelping from the two combatants inside. As Buck entered through the door, he heard the sound of the two animals fighting amidst the sounds of the horses whining, the cows bawling, and the chickens squawking. The noise was immense. Buck strained his eyes to see where the fighting was, and tried to find the string for the single light bulb that hung by the door. Finally his hand brushed the string, giving it a tug. When the light came on, the coyote had Turk by his right rear leg and was ripping it, with Turk yelping and trying to turn and get at the coyote. Not wanting to shoot fearing he would hit Turk, because of the very poor light, the two combatants faded further back into the barn, further back into the darkness. The coyote would not let up on Turk's leg. Buck's hands were shaking so badly he could hardly aim, but he knew he had to do something and quick. This was one big coyote.

Buck had tried to forget everything he was ever taught to do in the Marines, but now it was time to remember. Buck, barely able to see the two, turned and looked away. He then turned, leveling his rifle at the same time and caught sight of what he hoped was the coyote, and fired. He had learned on a reaction course with the Green Berets to shoot with your reactions, not your sights.

A yelp came from the darkness and then the Coyote ran limping into the light. Buck leveled the gun to shoot, but out of the darkness came one pissed off dog running on three legs. As the coyote turned to face Turk, Turk clamped his jaws around the throat of the coyote and with a few quick twists of Turk's head, the coyote dropped to the ground. Turk stood there still holding the throat of the coyote. Letting it go, he poked the head a couple times with his nose, looked up at Buck, and collapsed in a pool of blood that was beginning to spread out from under him.

Chapter Eight

Gracie, sitting in her easy chair, hearing what sounded like a car backfiring, put down the magazine she was reading, stood up and walked over to the front window. Not being able to see out the window, as they were steamed over, Gracie went to the front door. Flipping on the porch light and opening the front door, Gracie stood behind the storm door looking out to see if she could see anything or anyone. Seeing no trucks or cars on the road in front of her place, nor any distant headlights, she thought to herself, "That was no backfire."

Closing the front door, Gracie retreated to the kitchen. By the backdoor, she proceeded to put on her coveralls and insulated rubber boots. Throwing on a hat completed her wardrobe. Opening the backdoor, Gracie raced as fast as possible through the snow on the ground to her pickup truck. She opened the door and jumped into the truck and turned the key in the ignition. The engine barely turned over a couple of times, then nothing. Gracie dearly prayed, "Oh God, please don't let anything have happened to him." As she remembered, the last time she had talked to Buck he kept saying how he wished it were all over for him and how full of self pity he had been.

Gracie said a little prayer and tried the key again...nothing happened. Not even a click from the ignition.

"Damn, damn, damn!" she shouted as she pounded the steering wheel with both hands.

Gracie grabbed the door handle and jerked the door open and was immediately greeted by a blast of icy wind. With a shudder, Gracie climbed out of the truck and did the only thing she could...she started walking towards Buck's place.

Gracie pulled the ear-flaps down over her ears and tied the tie under her chin. Shoving her hands into her pockets, she felt her gloves and said, "Thank you God." Putting on her gloves as she passed through the front gate and onto the road up to Buck's, she thought, "God you know Bobby went off to Viet Nam, but Bobby didn't come home. Some guy named Buck came home that looked like bobby. I want my Bobby back."

As Gracie turned up the road she looked up and saw the light coming from his house and made that her focal point, not wanting to think of anything else, but could not help but remember another day she walked up this road.

She remembered how she had sat up in her room most of the day, first putting on one outfit, then changing her mind, would change into another. She was putting her hair up and then taking it down and putting it into a ponytail and then changing it again. She wanted everything to be just perfect because Bobby was coming home today. Her Bobby was coming home from the war. She remembered walking up this same road but it had been warm that day and she had to watch her pace, so as not to break out and perspire too much. She had only been on the porch with Billy and his mom a short while when they saw the dust from the pickup coming past Gracie's house. Bobby's mom had grabbed her hand and was squeezing it tightly. They were both bobbing up and down bending at the knees with excitement. Gracie glanced over at Billy and noticed a strange look on his face. He was looking out at the approaching truck with a blank look on his face and a sad look in his eyes. Then, the truck was at the gate and pulling into the front yard.

Gracie followed Bobby's mom down the steps and stopped short of where the truck stopped. Gracie noticed that Billy had stayed on the porch.

When the door opened and Bobby stepped out of the truck both, she and his mom stopped moving. Standing before them was the shell of the man they had last seen. His face was thin and his skin had a shallow look to it. But his eyes...his eyes were sunken and had a look, like he was looking right through you. There was no gleam to them anymore. They were like the eyes of a much older man.

His mom had reached out and hugged him and Gracie noticed his dad on the other side of the truck. He just shrugged his shoulders at her, and then she turned and with a big smile on her face, she hugged the man she had always loved. But, the hug she received back was not the one she had been expecting for over a year. It was more like one you would give to your sister.

She remembered walking to the porch and his mom saying how tired he must be and how glad she was to have him home. His very first words to any of them were to his brother. He said, "If you say one word about the war, I'll break your fucking neck."

It wasn't very much longer that he informed everyone that he was leaving. Not knowing where to, but he was going. He was gone for ten years with just a postcard sent now and then. But he never forgot his mom and dad's anniversary or their birthdays. He always sent a card, and it was always signed "Buck." Bobby never did come home.

As Gracie passed through the gate into the front yard, she first noticed the light coming from the front door that was standing partially open. She thought out loud, "Why is the front door open?" Her pace picked up a little, as she got closer to the door. She noticed dark stains in the snow coming down the steps. "Oh my God", she gasped and looked in the direction of the barn and saw a line of these stains leading to the open door of the barn. Gracie, knowing blood when she saw it from all the chickens she had butchered in her life, starting running toward the barn. On entering the barn, she saw a larger amount of blood in the light shining from the single bulb. She started screaming, "Bobby! Bobby, where are you? Bobby, what have you done…Oh God don't let this be happening." And then, she heard a voice say, "I'm up here, hurry!"

Gracie turned at the sound and started to run toward the house and saw Buck standing on the front porch. She ran as fast as she could in the snow, feeling the tears stinging her eyes as she crossed the front porch. She grabbed Buck and squeezing him as tightly as she could said, "Thank God you are alright." Then, leaning away, but not letting go if him, asked, "You are alright, aren't you?"

Buck, with an astonished look on his face replied, "Yes, I am alright. It's Turk that's hurt." Then, Buck looked around and asked, "How did you get up here?"

"I guess I ran up here. Stupid truck wouldn't start. After I heard the gunshot, I thought you…and that was all she could get out before she pressed her head into his chest and started bawling.

Buck held her for a moment until her sobbing slowed some and said, "You thought I had shot myself? What would make you think that?"

"Well, here lately you stay up here by yourself, and the last time you talked to me you kept saying how you wished the whole thing was over, and you don't care about me anymore, and damn it, I love you!" exclaimed Gracie exuberantly.

"So, you ran up here, all the way to help me…damn, woman, I didn't know you still cared that much. I have been staying away so as not to make a fool of myself." And with that, Buck pulled her to him and kissed her with all the passion that had built up over the years they had been apart.

Breaking apart from their embrace, Buck started to say something and then turned and looked toward the open door and said, "Can you help me? I need to get Turk to the vet. He's been mauled pretty badly."

As they went through the door, Gracie answered, "Of course I will. Where is he?" She then spotted Turk lying on the floor with feed sack bandages wrapping his lower half. As she noticed the blood was soaking through them, she exclaimed, "We need to get him to Ed's and fast. You grab Turk and I'll drive." With that, they rushed Turk to the vet and the healing began for all three of them.

Chapter Nine

As the months went by the healing had definitely taken hold. Bill had done an about face with his depression, and he and BJ were a family again. Of course you would almost have to include Chipper in the family, since it seemed like he was there more than at his own house. Buck and Gracie were seeing each other on a very regular basis, and everyone was saying what a cute couple they had always made. Everyone was glad they were back together and they both whole-heartedly agreed.

But Turk on the other hand hadn't fared so well. You would almost have to change his name to Tripod. No, he didn't lose his back leg, but Ed did have to put pins in his leg because the bones were so mangled. So now, when Turk sits, that one leg sticks straight out in front of him. When he runs, it sticks straight out to the side. He is still chasing that phantom rabbit, but his days of swimming in Gracie's pond are through.

Chapter Ten

As the winter waned its way to spring and a new life seemed to abound everywhere you looked, including the trees and lawns of every house that Bill passed on his way home. Bill couldn't help but look back over the last few months and think of the new life he had been granted. Sure he still missed Emily and there were times when he would slip back into slightly depressive moods. But with an uncountable amount of conversations with Paul, he began accepting that all that happens, good or bad, is in God's overall plan for him, and that you have a choice today to live with an attitude of gratitude for what you have, and not in self pity for what you don't have, and to count your blessings. Instead of thinking of how he lost Emily at such an early age, Bill was grateful for the time he did have with her and the memories...that no one could ever take away.

Then of course there was the greatest gift in his life, his son BJ. He had noticed a big change in him in the last few months. The biggest, was that his voice had changed to the deeper tones of a man. Bill once again had to thank Paul for making him realize how far he had wandered away from his own son. How he had shut him and everyone else out of his life. How different it was today.

With that thought, Bill was back to the present driving down Clay Road, past the park that used to bring him such pleasure when Emily was here, and such pain after she was taken. And today, through memories, the pleasure, although not as fulfilling, had returned.

As Bill was driving to his house, Buck and Gracie were on their way back from the grocery store in town. Gracie sat looking over at Buck as they drove along the gravel road leading from the highway to her house and then on beyond to Buck's. Buck turned his head toward Gracie and then back to the road and asked, "You have been staring at me for sometime now, something on your mind?"

"Well, first of all, I am not staring at you, just looking," Gracie answered. "And second?" Buck asked. "Something has been bothering me for some time, Bobby." She was cut off immediately when Buck's head snapped toward her and he asked, "Why can't you call me Buck like everyone else? Bobby no longer exists, and hasn't for a very long time." His voice was definitely harsher with the last three words.

"Okay...Buck, that's what I want to talk to you about. I want to know what happened to Bobby. Where did he go? I love you, sweetheart, but I need some answers. You're kind and sweet to me, but everybody else...seems like they're not even there, like they don't exist to you. I just wish you would open up and tell me what happened. I don't want to lose you again," Gracie said, as a tear ran from the corner of her eye.

Buck turned the truck into the drive to Gracie's house and parked next to the steps leading up to the front door. Buck just sat there with a blank stare on his face, looking out toward the distant hills. His mind was much more distant than the hills. For just an instant, Buck was in the back of a deuce and a half, heading north on Highway One, just north of Hue, the ancient imperial capital of Vietnam. It was mid August and hotter than hell, and he was standing next to Gunter, one of his best friends in the unit. Being basically new meat to the unit, they both stuck pretty close together. Up in the front of the truck they were just letting the wind blow through their hair and enjoying the coolness as they rolled along the road.

"Buck...Buck are you alright?" asked Gracie.

Buck kind of jumped at the intrusion into his daydream, and looked over at Gracie at the same time and answered, "Yeah...Yeah, I am fine. I was just remembering something from a long time ago." Then, he noticed the tears in Gracie's eyes, and reaching over he gently wiped them from her face. "I will tell you someday...soon I hope, but I don't think you will understand it. It is one of those things where they say, "You had to be there."

Buck helped Gracie carry her groceries into the house, and setting the last few things down, Gracie asked Buck, "Would you like to come up for supper tonight?" Looking up as she finished asking, she noticed Buck staring out the window and knew he wasn't there again. He was somewhere deep in his pain, and then he was back.

"I'm sorry. Did you say something?" asked Buck.

"I just said thank you for helping me, and that you look tired," she said, as she stood on her tiptoes and kissed him.

As Buck pulled out of Gracie's driveway, she said a silent prayer, "God please help him and all others like him."

Chapter Eleven

On his way to his own house Buck felt like he wasn't driving, more like he was riding with the wind blowing through the open window. Feeling his hair being whipped around by the air took him right back to another time, back to riding on that truck with Gunter. It was always little things that would bring him back to that dark period of his life, the part he wished so very many times he could just wash out of his memories.

As Buck turned in to his property, he saw Turk jump up from his napping place on the front porch and come down the front steps in his slow cautious way. Buck thought to himself, "I guess we all have our crosses to bear, even you Turk."

As Buck pulled up to the house, Turk had just made it to the ground, and then he put on the steam to be there when the truck door opened and his best friend stepped out. Buck opened the door and was greeted by the familiar barking and growling that was Turk's way of saying, "Hi, How are you? Glad your home, I love you, now where is my treat?" or something in that order. "Turk, you have let yourself become awfully spoiled," said Buck. Since Turk's surgery putting his leg back together, between Ed, the vet's assistant, and himself, Turk didn't go long between treats. Stepping out of the truck, Buck reached into his jacket pocket and produced a piece of jerky, Turk's favorite. Throwing it to Turk and watching him catch it and then lay down right where he caught it, Buck smiled as Turk began to devour his prize. Buck probably hadn't walked six paces before Turk was up and right behind him following Buck into the house.

Buck finished up the nightly chores, fixed and ate his dinner and cleaned up the kitchen before retiring to the comfort of his bed. Lying in his bed and looking at the picture of Gracie on the bedside table, realizing how much he loved her, Buck made a commitment to himself. "I will tell you as much as I can about what happened. I owe you that much." Then, he kissed her picture, turned off the light, and drifted off into another night of hell.

As the sun rose the next morning, Buck had finished his morning chores. Standing on the front porch, looking toward Gracie's place, he could see the light in a window and remembered his vow from last night. Looking down at Turk he said, "Could be a little while before I get back, so you will be better off staying outside." With a pat on Turk's head, Buck walked to his truck and drove slowly to Gracie's house.

Chapter Twelve

Gracie was standing at her kitchen sink finishing up the dishes when she saw Buck's truck coming down the road through her kitchen window. Seeing him turn into her drive, she quickly removed her apron and proceeded toward the front door, stopping at the hall mirror to fix her hair as much as possible. Opening the front door at the same time Buck arrived, she exclaimed, "You know, if you would put your phone back in your place, you could give a girl a little notice that you were coming by, and I..." Before she could finish, Buck grabbed her and kissed her with more passion than he had in a long, long time. "Okay, okay you don't have to give me notice...Wow, what's this all about?" asked Gracie.

"Last night, as I thought about what you said, about what happened, I realized that yes, you do have a right to know. I need to talk about it also. The counselors at the rehab centers push talking about it all the time. I love you, Gracie, and I don't want anything to come between us. So, if you have some coffee, I am willing to sit down and tell you as much as I can," said Buck.

Gracie made a fresh pot of coffee, poured two cups, and they sat at the kitchen table while Buck began. "Gracie, you have never seen, heard, or smelled the types of things I'm about to tell you, and for that, I truly thank God. As you know, I never drank any type of alcohol before I left. The night before we were to catch our flight to Nam, that is what we call Viet Nam, some of the guys in my unit were going to the E.M. Club on base. They wouldn't let us off base for fear of guys deserting. Anyway, that night, they asked me if I wanted to go. Gracie, I was so scared, not knowing if I would live or die. They taught us things like, don't drink the Cokes they sell on the street because the Gooks put poison and ground glass in them. Don't kick a dirt clod on the road because the Gooks put hand grenades in wet mud balls, and when they dry they pull the pins out so when you kick the dirtball it breaks apart, the handle comes off and explodes killing or maiming you or your buddy. Hell, they would do the same thing with a grenade and put it in the officers' showers and the water running down the drain would wash the mud off the grenade and the handle would come loose and explode, taking out whoever was in the shower. I am telling you these things to let you see that there was nowhere safe. There was no front line like in every other war we ever fought. It was total fear, twenty four hours a day."

"Honey, I don't mean to interrupt you, but what is a Gook?" asked Gracie.

"A Gook is the Viet Cong and the North Vietnamese Army. The people we were fighting. Of course you didn't know who was friendly and who was the enemy since the V.C. dressed just like the rest of the people. They didn't wear uniforms, so you treated all of them as the enemy. So, they were all Gooks. Anyway, like I was saying, we went up to the Enlisted Men's Club to shoot some pool, have a couple of sodas or beers, or whatever. One of my buddies, a guy named Gunter, was drinking a rum and Coke. He asked me if I would like one, said it would calm me down. I tasted some of his and ordered one. After a couple of those I wasn't scared anymore. In fact, I turned a complete about face. I became the baddest marine to ever set sail for Nam. I was going to kick ass and take names and come home a hero. I found my cure for fear…alcohol!

We flew out the next day on the same plane that some guys in Nam would be calling their freedom bird. I'll explain that later. We landed at Da Nang eighteen hours later. The fear was definitely back. The stewardess sprayed some kind of disinfectant or something all over the inside of the plane before they opened the door, and they did it very quickly. They wanted us off. The guys going home on it wanted to get the hell back in the air before a rocket or mortar round could kill them. I was about to go berserk sitting in that plane, wanting that door open and off that bird. I figured I was safer on the ground with some place to take cover if the shit hit the fan. Then, they opened the door…as long as I live I will never forget that heat that came blasting into that plane. It was very similar to when you open the oven door and you are standing right in front, just a wall of heat. We came down the ramp as fast as we could and the first thing I see is a line of body bags. That's what they put the guys that were killed in. Or as we said it, "Bought the farm."

The very next thing I see is these two Gook women selling cans of Coke. It scared me to death. One even came up to me and offered me one. I remember moving away from her quite rapidly and running into a group of soldiers that were on their way home. They kept hollering things like, 'New meat' and laughing an almost hysterical laugh. Their eyes…their eyes were empty, for a lack of a better description. They were looking at you, but not seeing you. It's so hard to explain some things, sorry," Buck said as he reached for his cup of coffee. Gracie couldn't help but notice his hand shaking. She reached over and held his other hand in both of hers.

Buck looked over at her and Gracie had never seen such pain in a person's eyes. "Baby, you don't have to tell me anymore if you don't want to!"

Buck just stared down at her for a few seconds and began again…"We had been in the country a few weeks and I had already seen so much carnage and desperation. I saw an old lady get her skull bashed in and killed over a little piece of plywood that was dumped out of a dump truck. The Sea Bees used to haul their lumber to the dump. We had drawn the duty to escort these guys, and I couldn't figure out why they needed an escort until I saw how the Gooks were swarming all over the truck. Even as it was still backing up and raising its bed to dump the scrap material, people were actually in the pile as it came out of the truck. The driver knew what he was doing all right. He never stopped backing up and dumping. Then, he was already going forward again and lowering the dump bed. That was when I saw the old lady come up from the pile with a piece of plywood that was no more than two feet wide and eighteen inches long. As she turned away to run...this kid, no more than fourteen, took a piece of board and crushed her skull. Then, scooped up the piece she had and started running with it. I raised my rifle to shoot him, but the older guys stopped me. One said, 'don't kill him...he's doing us a favor' and they all started laughing. I found out later, the reason they fought like that was because that's what they built their houses out of. I saw houses built out of the cardboard boxes the C-rations came in.

The only thing I found to keep me from going crazy through that year was booze and a little pot now and then. Gunter and I were as tight...no, tighter than brothers ever were. Men in combat have a bond that only men in combat can know.

Gunter was my best friend while I was in the service. We met at boot camp and like two peas in a pod we went through all of our training together, and then on to Nam. "You remember, I used to write to you about him and me?" Buck asked.

"Yeah, I remember, and then you stopped writing," answered Gracie.

Buck hadn't even heard Gracie's response, just went on talking. "Everybody in the squad called Gunter 'Gunner', since he was such a good shot, but not me. One day we were just north of Hue on Highway One. It was hot as usual and Gunter and myself were riding in the back of a deuce and a half. Sorry, that's what we called what you know as an Army truck, except it was open, with no tarp over the top. Anyway, we were riding along when we came to crossroads, and we stopped for this bus full of people to go by, mostly school kids. Not what you're thinking though. This bus had no windows or doors. It had a luggage rack on top where a lot of the kids, along with baskets of fruit and a pig rode. There were so many people on this bus. There were kids hanging off the side by the front and back doors. Anyway, this turned in front of us at this intersection and was moving along the road...when all of a sudden there was a loud explosion.

The next thing I remember is running toward that bus and trying to find a whole kid. There were arms, legs and torsos all over the place, but not one whole kid. I guess something snapped in me about that time. I went somewhere deep into myself. I suddenly didn't feel anything, good or bad. I just knew I needed a drink or some reefer or something. I just didn't care.

I thought, 'to hell with them, let them kill each other'. It was less than a month later, and again Gunter and I were standing up in the front of another deuce and a half and we were just coming up on another village. We were moving along slowly. Gunter had just told me that the thing he missed most was a toilet seat, dry toilet paper, and a Big Mac. Out of the corner of my eye, I saw a muzzle flash. Then, saw Gunter's face explode as the bullet took off his lower jaw and tongue. He was thrown into and on top of me as we fell to the floor of the truck. The truck came to a halt and the rest of the squad jumped off the truck and started firing into the trees and village. I rolled out from under Gunter and held him up to try to keep him from drowning in his own blood. But, he kept jerking around and coughing. I couldn't help him...and he died, not easily, like the movies show. My friend died hard for a nineteen-year-old man.

I don't remember getting off the truck, but I do remember going into that village, and I shot the first Gook I saw. Shot him right in the face. I have nightmares about that to this very day. I still see that Mamasan holding her little boy with no face and the blood running down the street like rainwater in a gutter.

Gracie, I don't make friends because they might be taken away from me. It's hard for me to sit by, while kids gripe about not wanting to eat what's on their plate, when I've seen kids picking through garbage and knocking maggots off something they found to eat. But mostly, I can't listen to grown ups who gripe about what they don't' have or don't have enough of.

Gracie…I hope this helps you answer some of the questions you had. I know I love you and want to be with you, I just…" Buck was cut off from finishing what he was going to say when Gracie stood up from her chair and leaned over and pulled Buck's head to her chest. In response, Buck wrapped his arms around her waist, and as Gracie kissed the top of his head repeatedly, she thought to herself, "Thank you God, thank you for sparing this man that I love so much."

Chapter Thirteen

At the same time that Buck was driving to Gracie's house, Bill was sitting in his kitchen having his first cup of coffee. Sitting there thinking back to when Bobby and he had gone on their first camping trip. They had gone to town with Dad to pick up some supplies at the feed store. Sitting on the counter of the store was a copy of "Boy's Life", the magazine of the Boy Scouts of America. Their dad was busy talking to Mr. Duke, the proprietor, so Bobby picked up the magazine and was looking through it. All of a sudden, Bobby turned to Bill and exclaimed, "Man, look at this, it shows you how to make fire without having to use matches." As it turned out, this issue had all kinds of stuff on camping, and the spark was lit for Bobby and me. Mr. Duke let us have that copy, and Bobby and I spent the next couple of weeks practicing different things out of the magazine any spare moment we had.

We truly had been bitten by the camping bug. Apparently Dad noticed our obsession and surprised us with a pup tent on my thirteenth birthday. I was so excited about getting that tent. I jumped up from the kitchen table where the cake and ice cream were and ran out of the house to start setting the tent up, when I heard Mom say, "What is this all about?" I remember my heart sank to my toes. Apparently Dad had not told Mom about buying the tent. When Dad explained to Mom all that had been going on with Bobby and I, she smiled, and I felt immediate relief. Then I heard the magic words as Dad continued talking to Mom, "And I figured since there isn't a whole lot to do around here right now, I 'd let the boys go camping tonight!"

Bobby and I were so excited that we grabbed each other and hugged, and Mom and Dad just laughed. Bill sat at the table and a sadness came over him as he said to himself "that was probably the last time we ever did hug each other."

BJ came walking into the kitchen about that time and said "Good morning Dad, what are you doing?"

"I was just sitting here thinking back to when I was a kid and me and your uncle would go camping" Bill answered.

"Boy, that's one thing I would like to try," said BJ, as he sat across from his Dad.

"Really, I didn't think kids did those kind of things anymore," Bill said with a questioning tone in his voice.

"Sure, me and Chipper saw this show on T.V. once all about the Boy Scouts and all the things they do, kind of cool!" answered BJ.

"Maybe we could go sometime, what do you think?" asked Bill.

"Really?" asked BJ excitedly.

Laughingly, Bill answered "Yes, and before you have to ask, Chipper can go too if it's alright with his parents."

BJ jumped up from the table, and running to his room started shouting "Chipper, Chipper, get up you lazy bones I have great news," and Bill started laughing and knew now why his parents were laughing that time at him and his brother.

Chapter Fourteen

A couple of weeks had passed, and of course Chipper's parents had granted him permission to go camping with Bill and BJ. Bill had even asked Chipper's dad if he would like to come along, figuring maybe they could become friends like the boys. Bill was definitely getting healthier, still missed Emily but had accepted the fact that he had to get on with his life. He sometimes felt like she was still there, and sometimes he would smile for no apparent reason. She would come to him in his dreams, not as much as she used to, but now when she came, it was as if she was there to be comforted, as well as to comfort. She would always be near, he knew that.

The three of them had made a few trips to the sporting goods store (Chipper's dad had declined, said he was to busy to go. Maybe that is what is wrong with kids today, this world has gotten too busy to take care of the real things that matter, like spending time with your kids. Believe it or not, they grow up and are gone before you know it! They had a pretty good inventory, probably more than they needed. BJ had even asked Bill to buy a back pack like the hikers use, said it might come in handy, so he did.

As June moved to July, and with a couple of camping trips behind them, usually ever other weekend, the boys had learned a lot from Bill. Even Bill was surprised at how much he remembered from those days spent with Bobby. He taught them how to build fire without matches, and to make sure you dig a shallow trench around your tent in case it rains, so the water won't run under your tent and get you wet, even though now-a-days tents come with floors in them. On the weekends when they didn't go camping, usually one night out of the week the boys would camp out in one of their backyards. Those two were inseparable. But Bill knew only too well how time and circumstances could separate any relationship, but nothing could ever take away the bonds of the heart, not even death. Bill was sitting in the front room when BJ came into the house, and seeing his Dad sitting on the couch looking down at the floor asked, "Hi Dad, everything all right?" Bill, sitting up straight, replied "Yeah son, just sitting here thinking about your uncle, I was thinking about calling him."

"Really, what brought that on? I mean you hardly even talk about him. I'm sorry, Dad, I shouldn't have said that" said BJ.

"No, that is quite alright, you're right, I don't talk about him. Seeing you and Chipper together, and my spending time with you two has made me aware that it is time for me to try to mend my relationship with my brother" said Bill.

Being a kid and not tied down with the heavy burden that pride can put on a person, BJ said "Gee Dad I don't see what the problem is, just pick up the phone and call him."

"It's not that easy, Son. First of all he doesn't have a phone, and second if I do find him he may not want to talk to me" said Bill.

"Like you always say to me, won't know till you try," BJ said with a smile and walked out of the room.

Bill, sitting there on the sofa, remembered what Paul had told him so many times, "You have to keep it simple, Bill" he would say, or another one was, "Nothing is the way you think it is." This got Bill to thinking that maybe it was different now, maybe Bobby would talk to him. Maybe Bobby was just as scared to call him, for fear of rejection. Fear of being rejected by another person could stifle a lifelong friendship. Fear is lack of faith, faith in God and that all things are in his hands. Paul had told him "When you find yourself being held back by fear, tell fear to stay where it was and ask God to walk with you."

Bill sat looking at the phone as if the receiver weighed a thousand pounds, and he knew he couldn't pick it up. After what seemed like hours, Bill picked up the phone and immediately set it back in its cradle, picked it up again, raised it to his ear and then set it back down. God, why is this so hard to do Bill thought.

"Lack of faith" seemed to leap into his thoughts, and Bill said out loud "God walk with me."

Bill lifted the receiver, and in his anxiety, dialed the old home number. With each ring of the phone Bill's heart seemed to race a little faster, then an answering machine came on "You have reached the Palmer residence, at the tone leave your name and number, have a wonderful day and God bless."

Bill pulled the phone from his ear and just stared at it for a few seconds and then gently hung it back up. Bill thought "God, if all things are in your hands, help me find a way to get in touch with Bobby!"

Just as fast as he asked, Gracie came to mind, followed closely with doubt. "What if she doesn't live there anymore, what if she got married and changed her name? Then what BJ said came to mind "Won't know till you try."

Chapter Fifteen

Bill got up from the couch, and walking back towards the kitchen, he heard the sound of children playing. Going to the kitchen window and looking out, he saw BJ and Chipper playing catch in the backyard. Bill was reminded of him and Bobby, always inseparable. If you saw one of the Stephens boys, it was a sure thing the other one wasn't far behind.

Something happened after Bill had decided to go to College instead of join up in some branch of the service. Bill came to believe that the Civil War wasn't the only war that put brother against brother.

One day Bill had walked into Bobby's room and told him that he had decided to go down to Kearny and start classes in College. The reaction he got from Bobby was exactly the opposite of what he had expected.

Bobby just turned around slowly in his room, and just looked at him, saying nothing for a few seconds. A look of total disbelief was on his face as he looked Bill up and down from head to feet. Then he said "I guess that kind of tells me which side of the fence you stand on, doesn't it!"

"What is that supposed to mean," asked Bill.

"You know exactly what I mean. This country has been free because we have fought to keep it free," snapped Bobby.

"Exactly what are you trying to say Bobby?" asked Bill.

"I have been watching the news, and I've seen what the colleges are doing to the kids...turning them into communists and hippies. I guess your going to be against the War and burn our flag and disrespect everybody like they do...right?" said Bobby with eyes glaring.

"Man, I don't know where you got all that from, I just want to go to college and make something of myself. I don't plan on being a farmer the rest of my life," answered Bill.

"Uh-huh, see what I mean, it is already happening, you are already turning against our way of living. You go ahead and be a big shot, I'll tell you what...no never mind, there is no telling you college boys anything. Except I will tell you this...as far as I'm concerned, you ain't no brother of mine!"

That was the way it was too! From that day on the Stephens boys were never seen together again unless it was with their parents. That wound never did heal.

Looking back out at the boys playing, Bill said out loud "Well, it is time for it to heal!" and he turned and walked back into the front room, picked up the phone, and without hesitation dialed information.

When the operator came on Bill said "Nebraska...Burwell." There was a pause and then the Burwell operator asked "What number please?"

"Yes, Maam! I'm trying to reach someone, but I don't know if this is the right last name, or if she still lives there or not" said Bill very rapidly.

With a chuckle in her voice the operator responded "Well, that is what I'm here for, the name please." "Oh...I'm sorry, of course you are, Gracie Parker, or probably Grace Parker in your book" answered Bill.

The operator told him to have a nice day, and a mechanical voice gave him the number. Bill immediately dialed the number and with each ring of the phone became more nervous. After the seventh ring and just about to hang up, he heard a familiar voice.

"Hello," said Gracie as she put the phone to her ear.

"Gracie, is that you?" asked Bill.

"Yes it is, who is this?" asked Gracie.

"It's Bill Stephens, how are you doing?" answered Bill.

There was a slight pause before an excited "Oh my God! I was just talking about you with Bobby. I'm fine, how are you?" answered Gracie.

"We are just fine. The reason I called is I need to talk to Bobby. Is he around there?" asked Bill.

"No Bill, you just missed him. He left about two hours ago. I really wish he were here," answered Gracie.

"When do you suppose you will see him again…I really need to talk to him Gracie?" asked Bill.

"That's really hard to say, Bill, he just got a job as a swamper on a rig going on a run to the west coast, and he just left. He said he would try to call me every now and then. I have no idea when though," answered Gracie.

"Are you sure everything is alright, Bill?" asked Gracie.

"Oh no…no there is nothing wrong, just wanted to talk to him, you know…try to resolve the problem we have. I just wanted to see if he would like some company this summer, thought BJ and I would come up for a week or so," answered Bill.

"That would be great, Bill, it has been so long, too long since I've seen you. It will also be nice to meet your son. How old is he now?" asked Gracie.

"He is thirteen now, fourteen the end of August, and he is the spitting image of his mother," answered Bill.

"I was so sorry to hear about your wife, didn't even hear about it till much later. Bobby wasn't what you would call very open about anything," said Gracie.

"How, has he been?" asked Bill.

"Well…where do I start. First of all, after he left the first time after he came home from the war, you were still here."

"Yeah, I remember," interrupted Bill.

"He would come home every other month or so, but you couldn't talk to him, most of the time he was drunk, and always angry, then the visits got further and further apart. Got to the point that nobody cared if he did come home. Of course, you know, he missed your parent's funeral, that was the last time I saw you, too!" said Gracie.

"Yeah, I know, weren't a lot of reasons to come up there, sorry Emily and BJ didn't make it up that time" said Bill.

"Anyway, it was ten years before he came back home. I guess he felt the same way you did. He doesn't say a lot about what he did or where he was, but I do know from bits and pieces of our conversations that most of it wasn't good. He is doing a lot better now, and we have been seeing each other on a pretty steady basis. Yes, before you ask, I still love him even after all this time and maybe some day, not soon, but some day, we may get married" said Gracie.

"Wow!...who would have ever guessed that skinny little girl down by the pond would someday be my sister-in-law. Congratulations!" exclaimed Bill. "That is just my hopeful heart talking, Bill, he has never even hinted verbally that he has any plans of that sort," said Gracie, with a chuckle in her voice.

"You guys have to be made for each other. Neither of you guys have ever married?" asked Bill.

"No, not that there haven't been offers, at least on my part. I don't know if Bobby ever had offers, he doesn't talk about his past very easily," answered Gracie.

"What about the farm, is he working it?" asked Bill.

"Lord no, the land is leased out to various ranchers or farmers to graze cattle or whatever, but no, it's just him and Turk, that's his dog, who is staying with me while Bobby's gone. Really a great dog, hangs around Bobby's during the day and stays here at night," said Gracie.

"Well, when you hear from Bobby, ask him to call me, please. Too much water has passed under the bridge, and tell him I love him," asked Bill.

"I will, you take care of yourself, okay?" said Gracie.

"I will, you too, Bye for now," said Bill.

"Good hearing from you, good bye," said Gracie.

Chapter Sixteen

Sitting at the dinner table that evening, something they rarely did, Bill asked BJ what he would like for his birthday. After a moment or two of thinking BJ replied.

"I can't think of anything I would like better than for me and you to spend my day at Astroworld. I would love to see you on some of those rides" answered BJ.

"Astroworld...I guess that could be arranged, but are sure you just want it to be you and me, what about Chipper?" asked Bill.

"No just you and me, I will explain it to Chipper!" answered BJ.

Bill watched as BJ got up from the table and walked to the sink to clean his plate and thought back to the day he was born. Finding it hard to believe that almost fourteen years had passed. Time is so swift at times.

"Is it all right if I go over to Chipper's and tell him, dad?" BJ said as he turned from the sink.

"Sure son…be gentle" Bill answered with a laugh.

BJ crossed the yard that separated their two homes and walked into Chipper's house without knocking (a practice accepted at both homes since both boys were at each others homes so much it was like they lived there) and walked into the kitchen where Ben and Mary, Chipper's parents, were sitting having a cup of coffee.

"Chipper around?" asked BJ.

"Well hello to you too" said Ben.

"I'm sorry, hi Mom, hi Dad (they were like his second parents and had been for years, Mary had held him many times when he needed to cry when he lost his mom, so now she basically was his mom. Where's Chipper at?" asked BJ.

"He just rode down to the store for me, he should be back anytime. Like a piece of cake while you wait?" asked Mary.

"No thank you, I just got through eating, maybe later if that's alright" answered BJ.

"If it's alright with you guys I will just wait out on the front porch for him" said BJ.

"That will be just fine, son" said Ben.

As BJ was sitting on the front porch waiting for Chipper to come home, Bill was sitting on the sofa when the phone rang.

"Hello" said Bill. "Bill, this is Paul, how are you doing?" asked Paul.

"Pretty good, what's up?" answered Bill.

"Well I just got off the phone with Bart Mercer over at Palmer Industries. That bid they are putting together has to be submitted a week earlier than they were originally told" said Paul.

"Okay, what does that have to do with us?" asked Bill.

"We have to get their blueprints finished so they can figure the amount of different materials they will need" answered Paul.

"So what are you saying Paul?" asked Bill.

"I'm afraid we are going to have to work our tails off, starting today" answered Paul.

"Today!" Bill said.

"Today!...how soon can you make it?" asked Paul.

"Well...in about forty-five minutes if the traffic is not too bad. How long do you want to work tonight?" asked Bill.

"If we work late, we might be able to finish tonight" answered Paul.

"Okay, I'm sure BJ can spend the night at his friends. I'll see you in a little while" said Bill.

"Just dress casual, only going to be me and you, probably" said Paul.

"Okay, Bye" said Bill.

"Bye" said Paul.

Bill hung up the phone and walked to his bedroom, went to his dresser and opened the middle drawer. Rummaging through his clothes to find a t-shirt he wanted to wear (something he rarely wore), Bill came across a manila envelope in the bottom of the drawer. Bill pulled the envelope out of the drawer. There was nothing on the envelope, no name or label. Bill straightened the little metal tabs and opened the flap. Looking inside caused Bill to catch his breath. Bill remembered immediately that Paul had suggested that he put some of the things, photos etc. away to help him recover. Inside was a poem that he had written for Emily. Bill removed the poem and read:

How Do I Know

When across the room a kiss is thrown
A tremor moves my every bone

Not like the roar of a thunderous crack
But as if a butterfly caressed my back

When. I walk so tall and grand
And people try to understand

Why I seem so proud and bold
They merely need to see your hand I hold

When in the night and all alone
We lie side by side our love is shown

We need not speak a single word
From heart to heart our message is heard

How do I know our love is real
It's not in words it's how I feel

How do I know our love is true
It's in your eyes when I look at you

Bill was totally oblivious to the tears on his cheeks while reading this. Upon ending, Bill wiped the tears away with his fingers and wiped his hand dry on his pants.

"I love you so much" said Bill softly.

Bill placed the poem back inside the envelope and pushed the flap over the metal tabs and started to bend the tab over when suddenly Bill thought "No…I'm okay with having this out!" and Bill removed the poem and laid it on his dresser top.

Bill pulled a t-shirt from the drawer, slipped it over his head and walked to the living room. Picking up the phone Bill dialed Chipper's house, and after a couple of rings Bill heard the familiar voice of Ben.

"Hey Ben, how you doing?" asked Bill.

"Pretty good Bill, how can I help you, do you need BJ?" answered Ben.

"Yeah, I would appreciate it" answered Bill. "He is just out front, I'll get him for you" said Ben.

"No, that's alright Ben, look I just got called into work, would it be alright if BJ spends the night? From what they tell me we will be working quite late" Bill said.

"Not a problem, I'll tell BJ" said Ben.

"No, that is alright, I'll tell him on my way out, thanks Ben" Bill said.

"See you later" Ben replied and hung up the phone.

Bill hung up the phone, checked his pocket for his keys and started for the door. Closing the door behind him, Bill turned to lock it and thought BJ might not have his key. Walking towards his car in the driveway he spotted BJ sitting on Chipper's front steps. As Bill walked up the sidewalk toward BJ, his son turned, and upon seeing his dad, a big smile crossed BJ's face. Bill's heart grew a size larger as he felt his son's love and the love he had for his son merge. Bill thought "I am truly blessed."

"Hi, Dad, did you need me?" asked BJ.

"Oh…I will always need you, Son, I just came over to tell you that Paul called me and I have to go into work" Bill said.

"But it's Saturday" BJ exclaimed.

"I know…something came up that we have to get done for one of our clients, I talked to Ben and he said it would be alright if you spent the night" Bill said.

"You going to have to work all night?" BJ asked.

"I don't think all night, but you will be asleep long before I get home from the way Paul talks" answered Bill.

"So what are you doing out here?" asked Bill.

"Waiting on Chipper…he had to go to the store for his mom" answered BJ.

"Well okay, got to go" said Bill, and with that BJ stood up from the bottom step that he had been sitting on and raised his arms to hug his dad.

Bill leaned over and wrapped his arms around his son's back and hugged his son a little firmer and a little longer than usual.

Separating, BJ said "I love you dad."

"I love you too Son" Bill said.

As Bill walked back to his car, turning up the driveway, Bill remembered the front door.

"BJ" Bill shouted.

"Yeah" BJ answered.

"Do you have your key to the house?" Bill yelled.

"Yes sir" BJ answered.

With a final wave Bill got in his car and drove to the office.

Chapter Seventeen

When Bill got to the office parking lot, Paul's car was already there. Walking into their office, he saw that Paul was hunched over one of the drawing tables.

"Good afternoon" Bill said.

"Hey, Bill, sorry about having to call you in, hope I didn't ruin any plans for you" Paul replied.

"Well you know me, had to cancel a couple of dates I had set up" Bill replied sarcastically.

Paul turned and looked at Bill.

"What?" Bill asked.

"Oh nothing…so how have you been doing?" asked Paul.

"I'm doing good…read a poem that I wrote for Emily shortly after we were married, had a rush of feelings come forward as I read it…but I'm okay" Bill answered with a smile.

"Yeah you are…I can see that in your eyes" Paul said.

The hours passed, one after the other, on into the early hours of the morning. Mindless of the time and the many, many cups of coffee, they came to one last page of prints to check for any mistakes.

"This is the last one" Paul said, as he rolled it out on the drawing table.

"Thank God for small favors" Bill replied.

"Something I do all the time, Bill, thanking God for all the little things in my life such as your friendship, the talent to do what I do…you ever have a child in the next car over at a stop light smile at you?" asked Paul.

"Well I'm sure I have, but what about it?" Bill asked.

"That is one of the things I thank God for. No matter how bad your day is going, a child's smile will brighten it, if only just a little. Having a thankful heart, filled with gratitude for the little things God gives us, that's the secret to a happy life" Paul replied.

"Paul, I want to thank you for all that you have helped me with" said Bill.

"No need to thank me, all I ask is that when you meet someone who is having a hard time resolving a problem that you have resolved, show them how to resolve their problem. What a wonderful world it would be if every person that mastered a problem could help two, just two, others master their problems. Why, dare I say, we might even achieve, world peace.

Paul turned away from Bill, looked down at the sheet on the drawing table, then turned back to Bill and said "I am going to give you something else that you can thank me for. Go home, I will finish this last one."

"Are you sure?" asked Bill.

"Definitely" answered Paul.

Bill looked up at the clock on the wall and seeing that it was almost three AM said "Well thank you Paul, guess I'll see you later."

Paul looked up from the drawing as Bill reached the office door "Take it easy, see you Monday. Thanks again for coming in."

Bill half turned in the door and gave Paul a wave and said "Goodnight."

Bill walked out into the open air and felt it's warmth encompass him. After being in the air conditioning all evening the warm air was very comforting. Bill thought about what Paul had said about having a happy heart, and when he thought about accomplishing the job they did tonight and how good the air felt, Bill's heart did feel a little happier.

Bill got to his car, unlocked the door and climbed in. He turned the key in the ignition and felt the immediate blast of cool air from the air conditioner. Reaching over he turned off the air conditioner and hit the buttons to roll all of the windows down. "The night is to nice too have the windows up" Bill thought.

He pulled out onto the street and was amazed at how silent the streets were. He couldn't remember the last time he had seen it like this. As he turned up on to the freeway the traffic was still very light, every now and then a tractor trailer would pass and he would wonder where it was going. Bill turned on the radio and tuned in a classic country station. With the air blowing his hair around and those old songs on the radio, he was briefly taken back to a simpler time. For just a moment or two, Bill was in the back of that old pickup truck of Dad's, riding along, with he and Bobby singing along with those very same songs. God, how he missed those days.

Bill pulled off the freeway onto Clay Road, and as he turned off the feeder, he was again amazed at how quite everything was. As he passed by the park, he said out loud "We never saw it like this, did we baby" and blew a silent kiss. At the same time his lips retracted from their pucker, Bill felt something lightly brush his cheek. Bill's right hand reached to see what it was, and for a few seconds he let his fingers rest on his cheek. Then he ever so quietly said "I love you too."

Bill was still holding his cheek as he noticed the green light ahead turn to amber, and he brought the car to a smooth stop just as the light turned to red. Bill shifted the transmission to neutral, returned his right hand to his cheek, then felt something cold against the left side of his neck just below his ear. As he started to turn to see what it was, he heard a thunderous explosion and felt searing heat. He didn't feel the bullet pass out just above his right ear.

Bill was above the traffic light when it turned back to green. There was no pain, only a calmness, a peace he had never known before. Bill looked down at the intersection and saw a hulk of a man reach inside his car and drag what was his body out around the front of the car and roll it into a shallow drainage ditch. Then the man climbed into the car and drove straight under him and away. As Bill was focusing on this unbelievable scene, he felt his left hand grasped by a smaller hand, and his fingers, like so many times before, curled around Emily's hand.

Chapter Eighteen

No one was awake at Chipper's house when the Police cruiser quietly pulled up to the curb in front of BJ's house. Officer Cambell climbed out of the patrol car, climbed the front steps and knocked on the door. Waiting a few seconds he searched for the door bell and rang it twice. With still no response, and following procedure, he left a door tag hooked around the door knob informing someone to call the Police station. Returning to his car Officer Cambell notified the dispatcher that no one was at the address, and that he would try again later if no one responded to his door tag.

Ben and Mary were sitting on their front porch having their morning coffee and enjoying the quiet Sunday morning. Both the boys, being teenagers, would be fast asleep for a few more hours. Ben had just turned to say something to Mary when he spotted the Police cruiser turn onto their street.

"First time I have seen one of those guys cruising through here in a while" said Ben. Looking up from the morning paper at Ben, and then following his gaze, Mary saw the car and replied "nice to know we are protected. All you read in the paper anymore is violence and crime."

As Mary finished speaking, the cruiser pulled slowly by the front of their house, and Ben gave a thumbs up sign to Officer Cambell. With no response from the officer, Ben's smile left his face and he said "He could have at least waved."

"He probably didn't notice you," Mary said as she returned to her paper.

"He looked right at me Mary…Mary he is stopping at Bill's house! exclaimed Ben.

They both sat and watched as the officer got out and walked up to the house, knocked on the door, waited a minute, and walked back down the steps.

"I wonder what's going on?" asked Mary.

"I don't know" said Ben.

They watched as the officer climbed back into his car, and were surprised when the vehicle started backing up.

Ben stood up as the cruiser stopped in front of their house and waited at the top of the steps as the officer got out of his car and walked up to them.

"Good morning, sir, I am Officer Cambell"

"Good morning, how can I help you?" asked Ben.

"I was wondering if you knew the family that live at 1711 Sycamore" asked Officer Cambell.

By this time Mary had arrived by Ben's side, "Well yes, we know them quite well, is there a problem officer?" asked Ben.

"Could you tell me where I might find the family?" asked Officer Cambell.

"Well, since there is nobody home, I assume Bill is still at work, he had to go in late last night, and BJ is upstairs, he spent the night with our son" answered Ben.

"And where would I find Mrs. Stephens, please?" asked Officer Cambell.

Ben started to answer "Well she…

"Emily was killed in an accident a little over a year ago, officer. What is this all about?" asked Mary.

Officer Cambell turned his head and looked down the street towards BJ's house, reached up and adjusted his hat on his head, then slowly looked back at the couple standing in front of him.

"I'm afraid we have a problem, I wish there was an easy way to say this…Bill Stephens body was found this morning, he had been shot and killed" said Officer Cambell.

Mary's right hand grabbed around Ben's left arm and, her left hand went to her mouth as she cried out "Oh my God, no!" as Ben stood their in shock.

"When, where…I don't understand…how could this happen?" asked Ben.

"How...how are we going to tell BJ, I have no idea...what do we say?" Mary was saying as Ben walked her back and sat her down in the porch chair and then sat down next to her.

Officer Cambell walked up on the porch and asked "Are there any other family members we could contact that could possibly tell him?"

"I don't know of any. BJ never spoke of anyone" answered Ben.

"How old is BJ?" asked Officer Cambell.

Mary looked up at the officer, tears streaming down her face and replied, "He is thirteen, just a baby, this is so horrible" and she leaned over, putting her face in her hands, and started crying. Ben put his arm around his wife's shoulder to comfort her.

"I can call and have a grief counselor come and tell him, it will only take a few...

"No...I'll tell him, I don't want a stranger delivering such tragic news, he is...almost like a son to me," said Ben, cutting off Officer Cambell.

"Guess I better get it over with" said Ben as he rose from his chair.

"I will go with you, honey, he is going to need me," said Mary, also rising.

"I'm going to need you too!" said Ben.

"I will just wait inside the door if its okay" said Officer Cambell.

Ben and Mary climbed slowly up the stairs, walking down the hall towards their son's room, side-by-side. Ben had his arm up around Mary's shoulder. More for support than to support. Ben said a short prayer "God please walk with me and give me strength."

Ben gently knocked on the door of the guest room where BJ was sleeping. Hearing no response, Ben opened the door slightly and looked in and saw BJ sleeping peacefully. A huge knot grew in Ben's throat when he looked back at Mary, she could see the tear wells growing in her husband's eyes. She squeezed his hand and nodded her head as they walked quietly into the room. Ben knelt down on one knee, reached over, and gently shook BJ's shoulder.

BJ had been in that state of sleep where you are asleep, but almost awake, so he just simply opened his eyes immediately. "Wow! what's going on, I didn't expect to see you two this…what's wrong?" BJ asked as his eyes focused more clearly on the pair."

"BJ," Ben started and then stopped.

"BJ, I'm afraid I have some bad news for you…"

BJ sat straight up in the bed and said "Is it dad? Please don't tell me my dad's been hurt!"

Mary sat down on the side of the bed, and Ben said "Son, your dad was killed last night." Officer Cambell could hear the scream from his place by the door, and he hung his head and cried. Mary grabbed BJ around the shoulders and held him tightly as he screamed over and over "No, No, No!"

Chapter Nineteen

BJ's screams and cries were only broken by the never ending question of "Are you sure, Are you sure?" BJ eventually pulled away from Mary and rolled over and sobbed face down in his pillow.

Mary stayed up in the room with BJ while Ben went downstairs and talked with Chipper, who was sitting in the living room with Officer Cambell. After a short while Officer Cambell stood up and said" I am truly sorry I had to bring this news to you, and I will do what I can to help BJ."

"I never really realized how hard your job is, having to do this all the time" said Ben. "It is never easy sir" replied Officer Cambell.

"What did you mean when you said "you would do what you could for BJ?"" asked Ben.

"I have to fill out a report about notifying the next of kin, and when there are no parents or legal guardians, the children are turned over to Child Protective Services. I know some people down there, might make it a little easier" answered Officer Cambell.

"Couldn't we keep him with us until we find out if there is any family?" asked Ben.

"Like I said, Sir, I will do everything I can to help. I'll see if he can stay for a little while, but no promises. said Officer Cambell.

Ben walked the officer to the door and they said there goodbyes.

Walking back into the living room Ben was greeted by Chipper with a strong hug. They stood there for a while in each others' arms.

Officer Cambell came by the next day and asked BJ some questions about his family. BJ told him about his Uncle Bob, but didn't know how to get in touch with him. Officer Cambell paid his condolences and told BJ he would do everything he could to find his Uncle. He also told Ben that he had talked to C.P.S., and his friend told him he would let BJ stay with them for two weeks, and if they didn't find any family he would have to go to a children's home.

The sun was shining brightly over the green lawns of Cottonwood Cemetery as the small funeral procession arrived at the graveside services. The different law offices had no luck locating Bob Stephens. They did find out where he lived. The Sheriff had gone by his place, and after talking to Gracie, reported back that he was unobtainable. That left only BJ, Ben and Mary, Chipper, and Paul Webb at the services. Paul was instrumental in the funeral arrangements. In the many talks Bill and he had, Bill had mentioned the plots he owned. There was a lot of unfinished business, but that could wait.

BJ stood as straight and tall as he could, not able to shed a tear as the wells were dry for now. Mary wiped at tears as Ben stood beside her with head bowed, his son stood between him and BJ, and Paul was at the end. As the Minister read the Psalms, Paul's mind left for a second. He was back at Blues Bar-B-Q, and he saw Bill sitting at their table, only this time his hand wasn't empty. He held hers.

As they were lowering his Dad's casket into the ground next to his Mother's grave, Chipper put his arm around BJ and said "I love you, buddy."

Chapter Twenty

Ben and Mary had decided not to tell the kids about the possibility of BJ being sent off to a home, hoping that BJ's Uncle would be found. They did not know that the search for Buck had been dropped by the officials. Gracie, not knowing Ben and Mary, and they not knowing her, had no communication. Gracie had called Bill's house a number of times until the phone had been turned off. No one lived there anymore. Gracie waited as long as she could for a call from Buck to inform him, but Buck wasn't the most reliable person when it came to calling. His past was proof of that. The days were passing way too fast. There were only two days left before the state would take BJ away.

Chipper walked into what was now BJ's room and saw BJ looking out the window. "Hey buddy, what are you doing?"

"Just thinking about Mom and Dad, wondering if all that stuff they say about heaven is true" BJ answered.

"Like what?" asked Chipper.

"Like do people get back together, you know like my Mom and Dad, Grandma and Grandpa. Can they see me? Are they angels?" answered BJ.

That's a lot of stuff I don't know about, but I did read, or hear about, that if you feel something brush your cheek and there isn't anything there, that its a kiss from an angel, Chipper said very proudly.

"Yeah right, like I believe that" BJ said.

"Oh yeah, I got to run to the store, want to ride with me?" asked Chipper.

"No, don't feel like going out right now" BJ answered.

"Okay, see you in a little bit," said Chipper as he went out the door.

BJ sat on the side of his bed and thought of what Chipper had said and wished desperately for something to touch his cheek. Tired of sitting, BJ laid back across his bed and drifted off to sleep. Chipper came back from the store, and finding BJ asleep, decided to go down and sit on the porch with his parents. As Chipper approached the screen door on the front door he could hear his parents talking.

"There really isn't anything we can do to stop it" Ben said.

"I know, the two weeks are almost up, I am going to miss him so much" Mary said.

"We may be able to visit him...really going to be hard on Chipper" Ben stated.

"Should we tell the boys or just wait till the lady from the state school comes to get BJ?" asked Mary.

With that, Chipper moved slowly away from the front door and snuck back up the stairs to his room and closed his door. Chipper walked to his dresser and looked in the mirror. "What do I do? Do I tell my buddy, or just sit back and let somebody take him away somewhere to some state school, whatever that is." Chipper started pacing the floor. "If I tell him, am I going against what my folks want. No...they said there wasn't anything they could do." Chipper sat on the edge of his bed. "What would BJ do if the roles were reversed? He would look out for me and tell me." With that in mind, Chipper went to BJ's room.

Walking into his room and quietly closing the door, after checking the hallway to see if the coast was clear, he turned around and was startled to see BJ standing there.

"What are you doing?" said BJ.

"Shhh!" said Chipper, holding his index finger to his lips.

"What?" BJ whispered.

"I overheard Mom and Dad talking. They were saying something about not being allowed to keep you, that some lady from a state school was coming in a couple of days to take you away" Chipper whispered.

"Why...I don't understand, why can't I stay here?" asked BJ.

"Probably some stupid law" said Chipper.

"Well I'm not going to any state school, I'm going to need your help" BJ said.

"What do you want me to do?" asked Chipper.

"Help me think of things I am going to need for a trip, I'm going to Nebraska to find my Uncle Bob. Like Dad told me, he is the only family I have" said BJ.

"That's a pretty big order" said Chipper

"I can't stay here. If I get put in one of those schools, I'll never get a chance to find my Uncle. I hear they are like prisons" stated BJ with a plea in his voice.

"Okay, I'll help you, lets get started" said Chipper

"I'm going to need my backpack from our camping trips, a map, a couple changes of clothes and a blanket. Can you think of anything else?" asked BJ.

"How long do you think it will take to get to your Uncle's?" asked Chipper

"I don't even know how many miles it is, maybe as much as five hundred" said BJ.

"If you walked four miles an hour, and you walk ten hours a day, that's a minimum of twelve and a half days. You're going to need some food!" exclaimed Chipper.

"Well, I'm not planning on walking all the way. I am planning on hitch-hiking" said BJ.

"I heard that could be dangerous" said Chipper

"When you don't have a choice, you don't have a choice, let's get packing" said BJ. The two of them started packing his backpack. The clothes, and a small blanket, some matches for making a campfire. They couldn't find a map, so they settled on an old geography book from school. They packed in a flashlight and Chipper thought of a must...toilet paper. The food could be a problem, so they finally decided it would be best to buy it along the way. A new problem...MONEY. Between the two of them they scrounged up fourteen dollars.

"I'll eat cheap if I have to, I'll work for food. Shouldn't have to, though" said BJ.

"I kind of wish I was going with you. When you planning on leaving?" asked Chipper. "I figure the sooner I get started the better, give me a head-start on that state lady. I'm going to leave tonight after your parents go to sleep" said BJ.

The rest of the day seemed to drag by. Dinner time came and the boys, wanting to avoid the parents, asked if they could eat up in BJ's room. This was denied, so they did their best to eat quickly without being obvious. Ben asked them once what they were up to. They both swallowed hard and said they just wanted to get back to a game they were playing.

Being a work night, Chipper's parents should be going to bed earlier than on a weekend night. Finally, the time came when Ben came into BJ's room and told both the boys goodnight. A little while later Mary did the same. Both times the boys pretended to be playing a card game. Both boys were too excited to sleep, so they talked or played board games. They made one raid on the fridge pretending to be bank robbers sneaking into a vault. This was also their test run for later that night. It was completely successful.

The time finally came. BJ put the backpack on over his shoulders, adjusted the straps and followed Chipper into the dark hallway. They had turned off the bedroom light before opening the door, but had to wait in the hallway for a moment to let their eyes adjust to the light. After what seemed like an eternity, they started moving down the hall. They got to the top of the stairs, and taking each step by placing both feet on the same step before moving to the next, they got to the bottom. They stood there for a few seconds and listened for any sounds coming from the parent's room. Hearing no sounds, they proceeded on with their secret mission.

The downstairs had some illumination from the street light next door. The closer they got to the front door, the lighter it became. Chipper slowly turned the deadbolt on the door, then turned the doorknob and opened the door slowly. There was a squeak that stopped them in their tracks. They looked at each other, stopped breathing, and listened. Nothing but silence. Chipper opened the door just enough to squeeze through and he was out.

"Come on, we almost have it made" Chipper whispered softly

As BJ started to go through, the backpack hung on the door causing it to open the door more, and that deafening squeak sounded again. BJ froze where he was, waiting for a light to come on, dooming him to a life in a state school. All remained quite. BJ shifted to his left and scurried through the door. He walked to where Chipper was standing on the porch and gave him a silent high five. They walked side-by-side to the front steps. Chipper looked at BJ and whispered "friends forever!"

Chapter Twenty-One

BJ stood on the front steps of Chipper's house looking down the dark street. With a lump the size of Texas in his throat, he could barely whisper "Tell you what dude, this might be a longer trip than I think!"

"I only wish I had more money to give you so you could take a bus or something, that's an awful long way to Nebraska," said chipper.

"Just do me a favor and tell your folks thanks for me, and don't tell them where I went. Make up a story like I went down to the ship channel and got on a ship or something. I can't go to that Child Protection place we heard your folks talking about. Just try to hold out for a couple of days, that should give me enough time to get out of Texas, at least!" said BJ.

Chipper held his hand out to shake with BJ, and BJ grabbed him and gave him a hug instead, "You stay cool, dude, and I'll write you as soon as I can, I promise" said BJ.

With that BJ turned and walked out to the sidewalk and turned down the street. Just before he passed out of the light of the streetlight, BJ turned and gave a wave back to Chipper and Chipper gave a wave back, neither boy seeing the tears in the others eyes.

"Well, its just you and me now!" said BJ talking to himself, as he walked along shifting his backpack to a more comfortable position (something he would be doing a lot before this journey was through). He thought to himself "I sure hope this geography book I had in class is up to date."

BJ made it to the freeway just as the rush hour was starting to slow down a little, if it ever did in Houston, and he started to wonder where he was going to stand to get a ride as it's against the law to hitchhike in the state of Texas on state highways.

That's about when he spotted his answer, standing in the median was a man holding a cardboard sign which read "Will work for food" and "GOD Bless you" was written below that.

All he had to do was find a piece of cardboard and make him up a sign. BJ spotted a small grocery store on the other side of the underpass of the freeway, a good place to get a cardboard box.

While in the store he thought to himself that it would probably be a good idea to stock up on some provisions for his trip, at least enough for a day or so. Being careful in his choices as to the weight and how fulfilling his food would be, he chose one of his favorite snacks, sardines and crackers. Taking his articles to the cashier and checking them through, the cashier asked "paper or plastic?" she was quite surprised when BJ replied "A cardboard box would be better, I need it for a school project, Geography!"

BJ packed away his food carefully, thinking how he had to be careful with his money as it may have to go a long way. Especially if Uncle Bob didn't want him there. Uncle Bob never did act like he liked him...he never acted like he liked anybody, even his dad.

As BJ was cutting out a section of the box, he was trying to come up with some catchy phrase that would get a ride as quickly as possible.

After a few minutes he finally figured if it was good enough for the pioneers it was good enough for him.

After a couple of hours of standing on the corner waving his sign at traffic, an old pickup pulled up in the parking lot behind him. An older man in an old battered cowboy hat leaned out the window and asked BJ. "What's your sign supposed to mean there, son?"

"Its like the pioneers sir, Nebraska or bust!" BJ answered.

"Well, son, you may want to redo your sign, from here it says Nebraska or but."

BJ quickly turned the sign around and noticed how the "S" was definitely lighter than the rest of the letters. Turning back to the old cowboy in the truck, his face a much brighter shade of crimson…"no wonder a lot of people drove by pointing and hollering at me" BJ exclaimed.

"Well son, I don't know why your taking such a chance hitchin' like you are, had to do it a time or two myself, but I was told by more than one of those drivers when I asked to pay them a little for their kindness, was to just pass it on, and give some other person in need a lift…so if you don't mind riding in "Old Blue" here, just throw your gear in the back and I'll get you as far as Centerville."

A grin that could melt your heart rose on BJ's face, "sure thing, Mister, right away!"

Climbing into "Old Blue" BJ said "Centerville, how far is that?"

"Well, I believe in first things first, my name is Jerry Fletcher, my friends call me "Bones.""

"I'm sorry, Mr. Fletcher, my name is Bill Stevens, Jr. My friends call me BJ."

BJ sat quietly looking out the window watching familiar landmarks go by. Looking up ahead just in time to see a sign that read "Huntsville 5" and below that "Dallas 210."

"How far is Centerville, is it the other side of Dallas?" asked BJ.

Bones just chuckled a little and said "Oh no, not that far, it gets its name from being half way between Houston and Dallas." "Mr. Fleming, I don't mean to be a pest, but how long before we get to Centerville? asked BJ.

"Well, first of all I would appreciate it if you would call me "Bones", and second, probably another hour and a half to two hours should get us there" answered Bones.

BJ sat looking at Bones for a few seconds until Bones looked over at BJ and then back at the road and then back at BJ and then asked BJ…"What?"

"My dad always said I should call all adults as Mr. or Miss out of respect, he always used to say "The way to get respect is to give respect" BJ replied.

"Sounds like your father is quite a smart man, that who you're on your way to meet up with BJ?" asked Bones.

BJ slowly turned and looked out the side window and quietly answered "No, my dad was killed a little over a month ago, my mother passed away over two years ago, and I am on my way to live with my uncle Bob on his ranch (at least I hope I am, BJ thought to himself).

"Sorry to hear that son, kind of a tough row to hoe for such a little fella like yourself; said Bones in a very soothing voice.

They sat quietly as "Old Blue" rolled along as mile marker after mile marker passed by and the afternoon turned towards evening.

BJ had fallen off to sleep as the scenery was changing from flatlands to short rolling hills, from hardly any trees to pine forests as far as the eye could see. When he awoke it was like a different world. Being raised in Houston, all his life he had only seen woods like these in movies and such.

Bones looked over at BJ and saw how excited BJ was and asked "What's the matter BJ, you look like a cat in a box full mice?"

And that is exactly what he looked like with his eyes looking everywhere and his head looking first out the right of the truck, then the left side then the back and back to the right, just as fast as a cat trying to catch all of the mice at the same time.

"Wow! This is awesome," exclaimed BJ in a very excited voice. Bones just looked round and thought to himself, what the hell is he talking about! "What are you talking about, BJ?" Bones asked. "The trees, Mr. Bones, the trees. They are everywhere. I have never in my entire life seen anything like this. It is so great!" exclaimed BJ. "Well, you have heard about 'The Big Piney' haven't you?" asked bones. "Yeah, we studied about it in Texas history last year. So, this is the 'The Big Piney', wow!" BJ answered. "No, this is just the western edge of it, it stretches from here all the way up to Shreveport and east over into Louisiana. Millions and millions of acres with towns and roads cut out of it" replied Bones. BJ sat looking out the window taking in all he could and Bones thought, oh to be a child again and full of wonder. A sigh passed his lips. BJ heard Bones sigh and turned and asked, "Is everything alright?" "Everything is exactly the way it's supposed to be" said Bones with a smile. "Well, not too much farther to my turnoff. It's about three miles to Centerville. I guess I'll just let you off at the gas station there" said Bones.

"Well, I really appreciate the ride, and I don't mean to be nosey, but how did you get your nickname?" BJ asked. Bones glanced over at BJ and then back at the road. "Got it a long time ago. I used to run the rodeo circuit and you can get a lot of broken bones riding rough stock. Bulls was my special talent. When I signed up, the rest of the hands knew they had to ride their best if they were going to beat me." Bones paused. "So, what happened? Why did you quit?" asked BJ. "Oh, I didn't quit. I was down in Dayton at their county fair/rodeo. I drew a bull named Terminator. He was the meanest, blackest devil you ever laid eyes on, but I needed a good ride, as I was tied with another cowboy that was awfully good. Well, they opened the chute when I nodded my head, and sixteen hundred pounds of boiling hell rolled out into the arena. We made the thunder our brother as we broke through the air, twisting and turning and leaping and jerking. That Bull tried to get rid of me, but I was tied to that devil with what we call a suicide knot," he said after another pause. "Well, what happened? Did you win?" BJ asked with eyes as big as saucers. "We rode out that buzzer and then some, and then Terminator won our personal battle. He bucked me off, but I couldn't get away. See, I was tied into that rigging with that suicide knot. I guess that made that old bull just that much madder, 'cause he went to running me into every fence and rail in the arena, stomped me, threw me over one side of him to the other side of him and finally up over his horns and gored me real bad. After all was said and done, they awarded me 'Best all around cowboy' and gave my wife that silver saddle. Well, looks like we came to the end of our trail. Here's the station," Bones said. Pulling into the gas station, Bones stopped "Old Blue" out near the highway well away from the pumps. Bones reached out his hand to BJ and shook BJ's hand. "Well young man, it's been a pleasure making your acquaintance, and may God watch over you in your travels." BJ opened the door and climbed out. He went to the back of the truck and pulled out his backpack and started to leave his sign, but looked up and saw Bones motioning him to take it. Grabbing his sign and stepping back from the truck as Bones pulled slowly out onto the highway, BJ waved goodbye and thought to himself, "May God walk with you too!" BJ turned to walk towards the station, and after a couple of steps he turned to take one last look at "Bones" and "Old Blue", but they were already out of sight. Looking both ways up and down the highway, BJ could see a few other vehicles, but not one old blue truck was to be seen. "Guess he was in a bigger hurry than I thought!" BJ said to himself.

BJ turned back toward the station, and upon approaching the door, realized he had never seen a door like this one on a store. It wasn't made of all glass like all the stores of gas stations he had been passing through all his life. This one actually had a doorknob you had to turn. It was wood halfway up, very well worn wood, and four windowpanes made up the top half. Grasping and turning the brass knob, BJ pushed the door open. Stepping up one step and entering the station, BJ found himself standing on a wooden floor, where you could actually see the paths made by the thousand of footsteps that had walked it. Looking up from the floor, BJ's eyes fell on a long counter, lined with jars of candy and gum with their independent mouths facing toward the customer. Anyone could reach in and get what they wanted. "This guy would go broke around my school," BJ thought to himself. As BJ walked slowly to the counter a gruff voice that stopped BJ dead in his tracks said, "Something I can help you with young man?" Startled, BJ looked around the store and seeing no one answered "Hello, Sir...I just wanted to buy a soda if I could," his voice growing softer as he finished.

Out of the shadows in the comer of the store stepped a man that no way matched the voice. Walking toward BJ was an old black man with hair as white as snow, and a full beard to match it. "I...I...I...," BJ tried to speak.

"Well, spit it out boy, look like you've seen a ghost" said the man now standing in front of him.

"I was just...I have never seen a store like this before, Sir, I was just trying to find the soda machine" answered BJ.

The old man looked BJ. up and down and then said "I was watchin' you from my spot there when you came in. I have pretty good ears for my age...I didn't hear you drive up. "How did you get here?"

BJ swallowed hard and replied "Mr. Bones dropped me off out by the highway."

"You hitchin boy?" the old man asked.

"Yes sir, see my Dad…

"Don't go tellin everybody your business lessen you know them, get in trouble that way!" the old man cut BJ off sharply.

"Yes sir…sorry sir" BJ replied.

"Soda water machine's in the front corner over there by the door" said the old man. BJ turned and looked, spotting a silver box with "Cold Drinks" written in red on the front. Walking towards it, BJ thought "I have never seen anything like this before." As BJ got to the front of the box he noticed a whirring noise coming from the box. Looking to the right and then the left, he saw some vents on the left side near the bottom. Putting his hand near the vents he could feel warm air blowing from the vents. On the front of the lid in the middle was a handle. BJ grabbed the handle and lifted on the handle but the door wouldn't open.

"You have to put your money in the slot to get it to open" said the old man now standing behind the counter.

BJ looked down to his right and saw the slot with a small plastic sign above it that read "25 cents."

Reaching into his jeans pocket, feeling his hand pass over the six one dollar bills he had, his fingers felt for a quarter in his change. Pulling a quarter from his pocket and dropping it into the slot BJ lifted on the lid. BJ stood there completely lost at what he saw. There were six rows of long slender glass bottles suspended in the air by silver strips of metal on either side of what looked like metal caps.

BJ turned and looked at the old man "You pick what you want, slide it to the left and lift it out" the old man said seeing the puzzled look on BJ's face.

Looking back into the box BJ read the caps. There was Coca-Cola, Pepsi-Cola, 7Up and then three he didn't recognize, Royal Crown Cola, Nehi Orange and Nehi Grape. The Grape sounded good.

"Is that Grape any good?" asked BJ without turning around.

"Best in the world" answered the old man.

Something in the way he said it made BJ turn and look at him and the old man was smiling.

BJ smiled and turned back to the box, slid a grape soda and lifted it from the box. Holding the bottle BJ automatically tried to twist the cap off.

"You have to use this opener" said the old man as he held the bottle opener out to BJ. BJ looked at the object in the old man's hand, walked up and handed the bottle to him. "What you going to tell me, a young man like you don't know how to use this?" asked the old man.

"No Sir, I have never even seen a bottle like that" exclaimed BJ.

The old man smiled and shook his head, opened the bottle, and handing it back to BJ said "Well, if you ain't never seen a bottle like this you're in for quite a treat."

BJ could smell the aroma of grapes long before he took a drink. The burst of flavor and the tingling of carbonation in his mouth was like nothing BJ had ever experienced.

"Wow!!, this is great!" exclaimed BJ with a broad smile on his face.

The old man laughed and said "Lordy, I ain't never seen a body light up so over a grape soda, my name is Robert Earl Johnson"

BJ. reached up and shook the hand offered him "Bill Stevens Junior, my friends call me BJ" said B. J.

"My friends call me "Cotton" said the old man.

"Nice to meet you, Sir" BJ replied, as he took another drink from the bottle.

BJ turned and walked over to the window. Looking out towards the highway he noticed that the sun had gone down. Turning back to the old man he asked "Mr. Cotton is there somewhere near here I could camp out for the night?"

"Well let me think...You could make camp down by the creek, or I guess I could let you stay behind my place here. If you decide to stay here, at least you would have a restroom to use and water to wash up with" answered Cotton.

"I would really appreciate it if I could stay here, wouldn't be any trouble, I promise" answered BJ.

Speaking of trouble, you ain't in no kind of trouble with the law are you?" asked Cotton.

"No, Sir, just traveling through" answered BJ.

"Well these days a man has to ask. You can spread your bedroll out on the back porch that way the roof will keep the dew off you, got to remember to stay as dry as possible, don't need to catch no cold" Said Cotton.

"Thank you, Mr. Cotton" said BJ.

"No need to thank me, BJ, I'm glad I can help you. that's the trouble with this world today, nobody wants to help nobody. People done forgot that the more you give the more you get back. You probably think I'm talking about material things, I'm not. I'm talking about things from the heart. You would be surprised how a smile or just a kind word can change someone's day, and it doesn't cost a thing. Try it sometime, you will be surprised how many times it is returned by other people. Now you get on out back and set up your stuff, just about dark" said Cotton.

"Yes, Sir, thank you, Sir" BJ replied.

BJ walked back out front carrying his grape soda, picked up his backpack and sign. Noticing that there was hardly any traffic on the road, he opened the front door and leaned in and asked "This isn't the Interstate 45, is it?"

Cotton looked up from whatever he was doing and answered "No, son, it's not, that's the Centerville Highway out front, used to be the main road people took to get from Houston to Dallas. Interstate's about three miles west of here. Interstate went through and just about made ghost towns out of a lot of small communities. Hotels, cafes, and a lot of gas stations went under, people that owned them moved out and went to work in the big cities, I guess."

"That is kind of sad" said BJ.

"Well that's change, boy…the Indians had a saying "All things change, even the stones", can't do anything but accept that as a fact. Only one thing to do when something comes along and knocks you down. Pick yourself up, dust yourself off and start all over again," Cotton said with a shrug of his shoulders.

"Well, goodnight, Mr. Cotton."

"Good night, BJ"

BJ walked around back of the station being careful not to step on or trip over anything as it was much darker. Trying to see became much easier when all of a sudden a light was turned on inside the station which illuminated the back porch. Walking up to the porch with more assurance, BJ noticed the back door had three boards nailed across it. "Guess it must be broken" BJ thought to himself.

BJ spread out his blanket and rolled up his jacket and laid it at the end of the blanket to use as a pillow. Sitting on the edge of the porch BJ rummaged through his pack and took out a can of sardines and some broken crackers. As BJ ate his evening meal under that pale yellow light coming from the window he listened to the sound of the crickets and frogs. He heard a hoot owl calling to the night and he thought of his dad and the camping trips. A shudder ran through his chest and his chin dropped down. Staring at the grass between his feet everything began to blur as tears filled his eyes. As visions of his mom and dad crossed his mind he softly said "I miss you so much."

Sleep didn't come easy for BJ. Between the mosquitoes and memories, he tossed and swatted all night.

The sound of chirping birds greeted BJ as he pulled the blanket off his head. The sun was just starting to shine through the trees making BJ squint his eyes. Sitting up BJ had one thought in mind, looking around, he thought "Where is the bathroom?"

Spotting a tall slender building with a door with a quarter moon cut in it, he thought "you have got to be kidding." BJ had seen pictures of outhouses in books and movies but never a real one. The closer he walked to the structure the more he noticed how dilapidated it was. The door was hanging by only one hinge and wasps flew in and out of it. Turning around and looking back at the station, BJ noticed everything looked old, even the porch looked like a strong wind would topple it. Weeds and small trees were growing up all around the outside of the building and boards covered all the windows. A sudden spasm reminded BJ what he came out here to do. Looking around again, BJ walked around the back of the outhouse and relieved himself.

BJ packed up his bedroll and slung the backpack over one shoulder and walked back around the front of the station. Walking up to the front door and grabbing the door knob, he found it locked. Stepping back BJ could barely make out a sign through a dirty window pane that read "CLOSED." Stepping back up on the step BJ wiped some of the dirt off one of the panes in the door and peered in. To his surprise from what he could see the store was empty except for some shelves that were covered in cobwebs and dust. BJ stepped back off the step and looking around thought "Was I dreaming all of this…must have!"

As BJ walked out to the highway the sun was just topping the trees behind the station and a twinkle of light reflected off a grape soda bottle laying next to the porch.

BJ stood beside the highway and looked to his left "That's the way I came from" and then to his right "So this is the way I'm headed." With that, BJ started the second day of his journey. As he started walking he remembered something his dad had taught him "Take one day at a time and treat each day as a new adventure." Looking behind him as he walked for any oncoming traffic, and seeing none, thought "Yeah, this is some adventure."

BJ walked for another hour or so and figured three or four miles. No more than five or six cars had passed him when he saw a sign in the distance. Walking closer he made out the number 75 and his pace picked up a beat. The closer he got to the familiar blue shield shaped sign with the white number on it, he noticed a smaller yellow square sign with a black arrow pointing to the left. This indicated that Interstate 75 was to the west of where he was standing and a shiver ran down his back. "That is what Mr. Cotton told me in my dream, he said it was three miles west of here" thought BJ.

BJ looked both ways (not that it was necessary, more out of habit) before crossing the highway. Hoping that his dream was right, BJ started walking at a renewed pace. After another hour had passed and seeing nothing in the distance BJ's pace was not much more than a crawl. The sun was almost directly over him and the heat was becoming unbearable. BJ had been walking along with his head down, watching the small clouds of dust kicked up with every step, when all of a sudden he was immersed in shade. Looking up he found himself walking under a giant live oak tree. "Thank you, God" said BJ Standing there he looked both ways down the road he was on and saw nothing but waves of heat and what looked like water sitting on the road in the distance.

Walking over to the trunk of the tree, BJ pulled the backpack off his shoulders and let it drop to the ground with a thud. Sitting down beside his pack be leaned back on the tree, licked his lips and thought "I guess we didn't think of everything after all." Looking around all BJ could see was miles of barbed wire fences and rolling fields of parched grass with a clump of trees every now and then. "I guess this ground needs some water too!" BJ thought to himself while reaching into his pack and pulling out a can of sardines and some crackers. Looking at the crackers he thought "I definitely don't need these right now!" BJ put his finger through the ring on the lid, pulled up, and pulled the lid back on the can being careful not to spill any of the oil that the sardines were packed in. Removing the lid from the can, BJ licked the oil from the lid. Turning the can up so the comer was at his lips BJ drank the oil from the can. Also, having no utensils and not wanting to use the crackers to dig out the sardines as he had last night, BJ thought "Dad always said a little dirt never hurt anybody" and dug into the can with his fingers. Using his index finger, BJ made sure to get every last piece of fish and, most importantly, every drop of oil from the can.

BJ had no sooner set the can down beside him when he heard the sound of an approaching vehicle. BJ tried to stand up quickly, but found that his legs rebelled with pain. BJ rolled over on his knees and hands and put first one foot under him and then the other and was able to stand up slowly that way. BJ was surprised when be turned towards the approaching vehicle that it was slowing down and stopping.

BJ watched as the pickup truck came to a halt right in front of him, and saw there were three people inside the cab. A man behind the wheel leaned around a young girl in the middle and a woman by the passenger door and said "What you doing way out here, boy?"

BJ's mind started racing as be remembered what Mr. Cotten had told him in his dream "Don't go telling everybody your business lessin you know them, get in trouble that way" and responded "just trying to get to the Interstate, Sir."

"Well how did you get way out here?" asked the man.

"I have been walking since this morning, sure could use a ride" answered BJ.

"I don't...

"Oh for Pete's sake, Fred, give the boy a ride, that is why we stopped" interrupted the woman.

"All right" said the man as he looked around BJ "Get your grip there and throw it in the back, we ain't got no room up here!"

"Thank you, folks" said BJ and turned around and picked up his backpack. Turning back towards the truck the young woman said "Which way are you going when you get to 75?"

"North" BJ answered

"Well we are going up to Fairfield if that will be any help" said the woman.

"Yes, Mamm, it would be much appreciated" answered BJ.

Climbing into the back of the truck BJ thought "I don't know where Fairfield is, but at least its north."

Settled into the back of the truck, BJ was surprised when about a mile down the road they turned onto the Interstate. Watching the miles roll by BJ was very grateful for the ride. He had learned a new respect for Henry Ford.

Chapter Twenty-Two

A little more than an hour had passed, and BJ noticed the truck slowing down and turning off the Interstate. The pickup pulled into a truck stop and came to a halt. The man called Fred leaned out the driver's side door and said "If you're still heading north, this is as far as we go, but if your going into Fairfield you're welcome to stay on."

"No, Sir, I'll be getting off here," said BJ as he grabbed his backpack and climbed off the truck. BJ no sooner got to the ground when the truck pulled away. BJ hollered "Thank You" and waved, and arms came out both sides of the truck and waved back.

BJ walked into the truck stop and went straight to the cooler and looked for a Nehi grape soda. Finding none, he grabbed a Dr. Pepper instead and walked to the cashier. An older man was ringing up another customer when BJ got to the counter. When it was his turn BJ asked "Do you have any Nehi grape?"

"Nehi grape son I haven't seen any Nehi anything since before you were born" answered the man behind the counter.

"But they used to make it, right?" asked BJ.

Another old man standing beside him at the counter overhearing the conversation said "Sure they did young man, but just like the little corner stores that used to sell it, the bigger companies pushed them out of the picture."

"Well, thank you, Sir" BJ said, and turned to the man behind the counter and asked, "How much do I owe you for this soda?"

"That will be forty-two cents with tax" answered the man.

BJ reached into his pocket and pulled out two quarters, handed them to the man, and waited for his change. As the man handed BJ his change he said "Have a good day." BJ turned towards the door, and after a couple of steps, turned and replied "May God watch over you in your travels through life," smiled and walked out the door.

The man behind the counter smiled back, turned and looked at the other man and said "I haven't heard anybody say that since old Bones used to pass through here, shame he died down there in Dayton."

BJ walked out around back of the truck stop where all the big rigs were parked. Standing there, he tried to figure out which way they were headed by the way they were coming in. He figured out that if they came in off the road from the exit they were more than likely heading north. If they came out from under the overpass they were headed south. After about a half an hour, he had picked out a couple of drivers that had pulled up to the pumps instead of parking their rigs out back like they were going to stay for awhile. BJ walked up to the first driver near the pump, a man that not only looked like he could whip a grizzly bear, but would probably eat him after. Had to be the biggest man he ever saw. Starting at the ground, this man had on a pair of scuffed cowboy boots, blue jeans, and a large wallet with a chain on it in his back pocket. The chain disappeared under the fold of flesh that hung over what BJ presumed was a belt. He had on a denim shirt with the sleeves cut off, and a beat up old straw cowboy hat on top.

BJ cleared his throat to talk when the big man hearing this turned and looked down at BJ. Anything BJ was thinking of saying was stifled when the big man said "What do you want, boy?"

"Well sir, I noticed you came up from the south and I figured you must be heading north, so…

"It ain't going to happen, boy!" said the big man, cutting BJ off before he could finish.

"I don't give rides to anybody, people ain't nothing but trouble, now get on out of here before you get run over or something" the big man finished with a snarl.

BJ turned and walked back to the store thinking he had better try his luck back out on the highway. Finding a shady spot beside the store and out of the way of customers, BJ set his backpack and sign down. Sitting down beside his pack and propping his back against the wall, BJ watched trucks come and go while he ate some crackers and washed them down with his soda.

Unknown to BJ the big man had watched him walk over and sit down. After he had finished filling up his rig he had parked it and went in to the restaurant. All the waitresses knew the big man, but only by his nickname, and they knew he was not the friendliest of customers. When he walked in they all hoped he wouldn't sit in their stations. Glenda lost out. Walking up from behind him she put on her best fake smile.

"Good afternoon, Bear, would you like to see a menu or do you want the special?" asked Glenda

"No, just bring me a couple of hamburgers and an order of fries, and bring me a cup of coffee now. I don't want to have to wait for my lunch very long, either!" answered Bear without looking up.

"I see you are your own sweet self today", replied, Glenda.

Looking up at Glenda "I'm sorry, just the way I am" said Bear.

While Bear was drinking his coffee while waiting for his food to get there, he spotted BJ sitting by the back of the store. As he watched BJ eating his crackers, he starting reflecting on his own childhood. He remembered how at fifteen he packed his bags and moved out of the last foster home he was ever going to live in. He started remembering all the people he had met over the last eighteen years. How the only home he had was that old truck, and that was fine with him. Watching the young boy out there reminded him a lot of himself. When Glenda came with his lunch, he asked her to make a couple of hamburgers for him to take with him. When he asked for these again, he didn't look up, and Glenda followed his gaze to the boy eating crackers.

"There might be a place for you in heaven after all" said Glenda as she walked away.

"Say what?" Bear said, but she was already gone.

Bear ate his lunch, occasionally looking up and watching the boy outside. Walking up to the cash register Bear made eye contact with Glenda who met him at the register.

"It will be just a moment or so for your burgers, wanted to make sure they were hot" said Glenda.

"Thank you, I appreciate that" said Bear.

Bear paid for the food and excused himself to use the restroom "I will pick those burgers up on my way out."

During the time Bear left the table, paid for his food, used the restroom and made it back outside, the boy was already gone.

Walking out the door Bear looked over to where the boy had been. Not seeing him, Bear walked around the back of the store to see if he could find him. Looking around the parking area and not finding him, Bear headed for his rig. Climbing up in his rig and standing by the door he made one last scan of the area, seeing nothing, he threw the burgers on the passenger seat and climbed in.

Sitting behind the wheel still parked in the line with the other trucks, Bear looked over at the sack on the other seat and said to himself "Man what has come over you." Bear put the rig in gear and pulled out of the truck stop on to the road along the interstate. Looking up ahead Bear spotted a familiar sight, no not BJ, he saw himself walking along a lonely highway. Bear pulled up to the stop sign at the intersection where the traffic passed under the overpass and stopped. Blowing his air horns, he got BJ's attention. BJ was a good two hundred yards on the other side of the intersection when the rig pulled up beside him and stopped.

BJ climbed up the steps on the rig and opened the door. "Did you change your mind, Mister?" asked BJ with a big smile on his face.

"No, I just thought you might like a couple of hamburgers. I bought them for you, and when I came out back you were already gone. Go ahead and take them" Bear said pointing to the sack on the seat.

"Thanks anyway, Mister" said BJ as the smile left his face and he started to climb back down the steps.

"The names Bear…climb on in," said Bear as he shook his head, not believing he was doing this.

"Really, are you sure?" said BJ as he climbed in to the rig. Grabbing the sack off the seat, BJ sat down and shut the door with a resounding slam.

"Wow, this is just too cool, I have never sat in a big rig, much less get to ride in one, this is probably one of the coolest things I have ever…

"Whoa, whoa, whoa let's stop right there" Bear interrupted BJ.

"First of all there are a couple of rules, you don't smoke do you?" BJ shook his head. "That's good, cause there ain't no smoking inside Wendy, that's my rig's name, me and her been together almost eight years now. Second I don't want you jabbering all the time, I like it quiet. Think you can do that?" asked Bear.

"Yes sir, Mister Bear" BJ answered.

"There ain't no mister, it's just Bear."

"I know, Sir, but I was brought up…" BJ saw the look in Bears eyes and put his thumb and index finger to his lips and made a locking motion.

"That's better," said Bear, as he checked the drivers side mirror and pulled off the shoulder onto the road.

Pulling off the on-ramp onto the freeway bear asked "How far are you going?"

Silence.

Bear looked over at BJ and said "It is okay for you to answer my questions."

"I met a man that told me I shouldn't tell people my business unless I knew them" answered BJ.

"Fine, just do me a favor, tell me what state your going to so I don't have to wonder all the way when all of a sudden you start hollering you need off" Bear asked through clinched teeth.

"Nebraska" BJ answered

"Well I'm sorry to say I'm not going that far. I will take you as far as Pauls Valley, that is about half way through Oklahoma. So kick back and relax." said Bear.

Chapter Twenty-Three

The pair rode along in silence, interrupted occasionally when another trucker would come across the CB radio asking for information, directions, or mostly they wanted to know about Bears. Not knowing the CB lingo, BJ was completely confused.

"Excuse me, can I ask you a question?" asked BJ.

"I guess if you have to!" said Bear.

"I keep hearing all this talk about bears. That one guy was even saying there were a couple of Bears back at that truck stop we came from" said BJ.

Bear grinned and let out a little chuckle "How old are you boy?" asked Bear

"I'm fourteen, my birthday was last month" answered BJ.

"Fourteen huh, that's about the same age I was when I hit the road" said Bear and then he sat there in silence until BJ asked him again.

"What about the Bears?" asked BJ.

Bear seemed to snap out of a trance as he jumped slightly at the sound of BJ's voice.

"Sorry about that, I was just remembering back to when I was your age. Bears are the State Troopers. We have a different name for a lot of things. County Mounty is a Sheriff, and a City Kitty is, of course, a city cop. You might hear for example "We got a Bear at marker 120 taking pictures and giving out Green stamps" that means there is a State Trooper near mile marker 120 using his radar and giving out speeding tickets."

"That's kind of cool, so you truckers kind of have your own language" said BJ.

Reaching over to the knob on the radio Bear asked "I guess you probably don't like country music, but that is what me and Wendy like."

"Actually I like all types of music, Country is my favorite" said BJ.

"Oh really!" said Bear with a surprised look on his face.

"Yeah really, I have been brought up listening to Country. That is all my dad listened to on the radio in his car," BJ answered, and turned and looked out the side window.

The pair drove along listening to the radio. Every now and then Bear would sing along with part of a song he knew. BJ sat quietly listening, reflecting on how his dad did the same thing.

"Say, when you going to eat those hamburgers I bought you?" Bear asked. BJ had completely forgotten about them in his excitement of getting this ride. Bending over and picking up the sack from the floor in front of his seat, BJ asked "So you started out on the road when you were a kid, too?"

Bear looked over at BJ and watched as he started unwrapping the burger. He looked back out the window and stated "Yes, young man, I did." My parents were killed in a head-on collision when I was nine years old. Being an only child of parents that had no brothers or sisters, and both sets of grandparents gone, the State of Ohio put me in a foster care system. I had some good foster parents, and I had some not so good foster parents. The older I got, I realized I was never going to be adopted. Most people want babies or toddlers. Older kids need love and stability too.

Anyway, I was in with this family that had a farm out in Lawrence County, and I swear the animals had it better. All I was allowed to do was go to school, and that was because the State required it, and work the rest of the time around that farm. That family only took in kids that were older and males. The State thought it was a blessing as they could place older kids, and they didn't have to mess with them. This family is still getting away with, what I like to call, slave labor.

Like I said earlier, when I was fifteen I packed my bags and left that farm. I didn't know where or what I was going to do, just knew there had to be something better. I have been traveling around this country for eighteen years now."

"Yeah I heard about those State schools" said BJ.

"So what's up with you, where are your parents?" asked Bear.

BJ thought for a moment whether to tell the truth or not, "Kind of like you, they are both dead, but I'm on my way to my Uncle's."

"Well that's good that you still have family. Your Uncle must be looking forward to seeing you." said Bear.

"Yeah," BJ answered.

Just as BJ answered, George Jones came on the radio and Bear started singing "He stopped loving her today" along with the radio. BJ was glad that part of the conversation was over.

They had been riding along in silence for awhile when all of a sudden Bear blurted out "Here comes the Corsicana Curve."

"What are you talking about?" said BJ looking up ahead.

"The Corsicana Curve", coming out of Galveston all the way to Corsicana, it's a straight shot due north until you get to this curve up ahead" said Bear.

BJ looked up ahead and he could see a ninety degree right turn in the freeway.

"Yeah, you don't want to be half asleep at night when you hit this curve" said Bear.

BJ sat beside Bear and watched as Bear geared down and maneuvered that big rig around that curve and geared back up to speed, a real piece of art.

"You are really good!" said BJ.

"Lots of practice over lots of curves, kind of like life, boy. Learn from your mistakes, those so-called bumps and bruises life hands us. Make your life a whole lot smoother" replied Bear.

Not much further there was another curve to the left this time, a whole lot more gradual, and they were heading due north again. As they passed Corsicana, BJ noticed the terrain changing from flat land to rolling hills. They were in a convoy with five other trucks, and they were all chattering over their CBs.

"You know, Bear, sounds to me like you know an awful lot of these guys" BJ exclaimed. Yeah, I have made a lot of friends over the years. Whenever I find one of my buddies on the radio, we usually have a lot to talk about, like where they have been hauling, who they saw or talked to, that kind of stuff" said Bear.

"Sure got hilly all of sudden" said BJ.

"Changes all the time, we will be in hills all the way to Dallas, then it gets flat up to the Red river." said Bear

"The red river, that's the state line right?" asked BJ.

"That's right, we cross that bridge and we are in Oklahoma" said Bear.

BJ watched as the hills started losing their wonder and became kind of boring, when, all of a sudden, as they came over the top of the hill. "WOW!" exclaimed BJ loudly.

Bear let out a loud laugh and said "I always like to surprise people with that!"

Stretched out before BJ's eyes just like magic was 'Dallas Texas', there was no warning. You are in hills that hide the skyline, and until you top that last hill, you don't see it and then there it is. Just like in the TV series you come in on those two bridges that are side by side. One heading north and one heading south. Before BJ could catch his composure they were on the bridge and Dallas' skyline was rushing towards them.

"Okay now, when we get into Dallas I have a couple of tricky interconnects to make, the first onto 35 West, so I need concentrate. Do you understand what I'm saying, boy?" stated Bear.

"Yeah, you want me to keep my trap shut" answered B.J

"Well, yeah something like that, by the way, you do have a name don't you?" asked Bear

"Yeah, my friends call me BJ."

BJ was in awe once again as Bear worked his magic as they went through the interconnect where I-45, I-20 and I-35 crisscrossed each other with some very quick lane changes involved. The next thing BJ knew he was dead smack in the middle of downtown Dallas on I-35 heading north once again.

Bear let out a long sigh and said "Boy I am glad that one's behind us. Oklahoma City is a piece of cake compared to Dallas!"

"Will I still be with you in Oklahoma City?" asked BJ.

"Well, no you won't, see Pauls Valley comes before Oklahoma City, I was just making a point, BJ" answered Bear.

"Oh yeah, I get it…I guess Oklahoma City is smaller than Dallas, right?" asked BJ.

"Yeah, and a lot simpler to pass through, remember, all you have to do is stay on 35 and it will take you around the city and straight up through Wichita Kansas" answered Bear.

"Boy, you really know your roads!" stated BJ.

"Been running these roads a long time," and then the pair fell off into silence as the Dallas skyline fell behind them.

Chapter Twenty-Four

At the same time Bear's rig was heading north through Irving Texas, the rig Buck had been working out of was heading east out of Taylor Nebraska, just seven miles from home.

"Boy, it's sure good to be getting back home again. Funny, this is the first time in a long time I have felt this way" said Buck.

"You did a good job for me, Buck, really starting to get the hang of this old rig of mine too. Sure could use a man like you. What would you think about running with me full time?" asked Red.

"Really!!...That would be great!" answered Buck with a big grin on his face.

"I got a run in a couple of days down to Sarasota, Florida if you would be interested?"

"If I'm going to be full-time, just let me know when we are leaving" answered Buck as he reached across and shook Red's hand.

Red put the right turn signal on as he approached the turnoff on to the road to Buck's place. "I'm sure your going to be glad to see Gracie" said Red.

"That's a big 10-4" replied Buck.

"I just can't figure out why you never called her while we were out" said Red.

"I'm just not much on phones, Red, just seems so…I don't know, when you talk to somebody, I like to see their eyes and expressions…really hard to explain" said Buck.

As they approached Gracie's house, Buck asked Red to blast the air horns and he did.

Gracie was bent over her laundry basket pulling a bed sheet out when she was startled by the blaring sound of the horn, causing her to jump up straight and throw clothes pins all over the backyard. Turk, who had stayed at her house today, jumped up from his place in the shade and ran around the side of the house and stopped as the big rig passed by the front of the house. Gracie caught up with Turk just as the back of the trailer went by her driveway. Red just caught a glimpse of Gracie coming around the corner and stuck out his arm and waved and blasted the horn three more times. Turk took off on a dead run, three legs on the ground and the fourth sticking straight out in the rear.

Gracie ran in to the kitchen and grabbed her keys off the counter and raced back to her truck. As she climbed in and started the truck, she remembered what she had to tell Buck, and everything slowed down including her heartbeat. She put the truck into reverse and backed down her driveway onto the road facing Buck's place. "How do I start?" she thought to herself. Gracie was about two thirds of the way to Buck's when she came up on Turk sitting beside the road. Gracie stopped the truck and leaned over and opened the door and Turk jumped in and sat down on the passenger side. He turned and looked at Gracie and gave a muffled bark and looked back toward the front.

"Well you're welcome" said Gracie and took of rapidly enough to cause the door to close.

As Gracie drew closer to Buck's place, the rig was pulling away from the main gate, and as the trailer cleared the view of the house, she saw Buck walking towards the house and a hitch came in her throat. A combination of her love for him and sadness for the message she was bringing caused a flood of tears to rush down her cheeks, some she wiped away with her hand, some fell on her blouse. Turk was up and was trying to get out the window as the truck approached the gate. Turk turned back towards Gracie, and whining, with tail wagging and quiet little barks, was showing his anxiety to get to his master and friend. As the truck turned in below the rocking Bs sign and crossed the cattle guard, Buck turned and waved with his free hand, the other carrying his traveling bag. Turk could hold back no longer and was airborne, out through the window he went, landing on the run, and was at full speed when he hit the ground on his three good legs. Buck seeing Turk coming hurried to the front steps at a full run and set his bag down just as Turk leapt up and Buck caught his front paws in his arms. Gracie drove slowly up through the front yard witnessing the greeting that pair was giving each other. The unconditional love those two had was showing, and then something caught her eye. Yes it was, every now and then as the pair wrestled and jumped around, she saw Bobby peak out of Buck, and she smiled.

Gracie parked the truck and climbed out the driver's side and walked around the front of the truck. Buck stopped wrestling with Turk and looked over at Gracie and said "God, you would think I have been gone for..."and then Buck noticed the tears in Gracie's eyes. "Baby, did you miss me that much, too?" and the dam really broke as Gracie hurried into Buck's arms and they hugged. Then Buck pushed away just enough to kiss Gracie, first gently, and then a longer, more passionate kiss. Then as Buck held her tightly to his chest he felt the sobs coming from Gracie and held her at arms length.

"Baby, is everything alright? I was going to call if we were going to be out any longer, but..."

"No, no that's not it. I have some bad news, and I have been waiting so long to hear from you to let you know," Gracie said quietly through sobs.

"What is it Baby?" said Buck as he held Gracie's shoulders.

"Its your brother…Bobby…Bill was killed!" Gracie barely got the last word out before she burst out crying.

Buck's hands fell from Gracie's shoulders and a blank stare came over his face. He was looking at Gracie but not seeing her, and then his legs seemed to give way and he just sat down on the ground. Turk walked up beside Buck and sat down beside him. Buck reached out and put his arm around Turk's shoulders and just sat there. Buck's mind left him as he traveled through time, back to the pond, wrestling on their bed as kids, standing arm-in-arm admiring the job they did on the chicken coop. Then it moved forward to Billy helping him with his homework in High School, and then the argument about him going to college and the war. Then flashed forward once more to when Billy brought Emily home from college, and how happy he had seen them together.

Gracie sat down beside Buck and put her hand in his and held it, and Buck's mind returned to the present.

"When?" Buck asked softly.

"The Sheriff came by a little over two weeks ago, you had been gone just a day or so. He came by looking for you at my place after not finding you home. He didn't have a lot of details." answered Gracie.

"They didn't tell you what happened…you said he was killed!" Buck said as his voice took on a harshness Gracie recognized.

"All the Sheriff told me was that he had been shot, I don't know anything else. I'm so sorry" Gracie said.

Buck looked away from Gracie and raised his face towards the sky and a look of hatred came over his face. "Why…why everybody else in my family, why do you hate me so much…Oh God, what did I ever do!!!" Buck was standing with his fists raised in the air and shouted at the top of his lungs "I HATE YOU MORE!"!! and ran away with Turk in close pursuit.

Gracie sat on the front steps, knowing he needed to he alone, but wanting to be with him at the same time. She glanced around the farm and everywhere she looked she couldn't help but feel herself being pulled back in time, but when her eyes gazed at the pond, her mind's eye saw two little boys wearing paper pirate hats and laughing as they threw dirt clods at a board out in the water.

"God, why does it have to change, life used to be so simple…I love him, God, please watch over him. I know, and you know, he is really a good man. Please help him" Gracie said silently to herself.

A little over an hour had passed when Gracie saw Turk come from around the back of the house. Turk walked straight up to Gracie and whined and turned back towards the way he had come.

"What's the matter, boy?" asked Gracie.

Turk walked a couple of steps and whined a couple of times.

Gracie stood up from the steps and taking a step towards Turk saw him walk back towards the corner of the house. Following Turk as he led her over a small rise, Gracie suddenly realized where they were heading. As the pair approached the family cemetery plot that sat on a small hill behind the house, Gracie saw the man she loved sitting beside his mother's tombstone. Gracie walked slowly towards Buck and waited a short distance from him until he looked up at her. She could see that Buck had been crying from the redness of his eyes.

"Be okay if I sit with you, or do you still want to be alone?" asked Gracie gently.

Buck only looked at her and raised his arm in her direction. Gracie walked over and sat down beside him and leaned her head onto his shoulder as he wrapped his arm around her.

They sat there for another half hour before Buck said "I have been alone much too long, I have come to the conclusion that life is much too short, as now my brother has shown me. I was sitting up here talking to my parents about my life and all that I have lost when I guess I fell asleep. Gracie…I had the strangest dream. I was sitting here, and Mom, Dad, Emily and Bill were all sitting here with me, and they all said the same thing. They said "God loves you, and it is okay." Then they each stood up one at a time and walked over and put their hand on either my cheek or my shoulder."

"Maybe it wasn't a dream after all Bobby…Gracie started to say, when Buck cut her off.

"It was a dream, alright, because then this old Black man came walking up from somewhere and said "Take care of him" and then he just turned around and was gone. I have no idea what that was about. When I woke up, I felt a little better."

"Well I am glad to hear your doing a little better, you ready to walk back down to the house?" asked Gracie.

With a nod of his head, the pair stood up and the three of them walked back to the house.

Chapter Twenty-Five

BJ had nodded off in the passenger seat as the rig rolled north on 35. Bear would glance over every now and then and just smile. "Sure is a good little fella" Bear thought to himself.

Coming up to the Gainsville exit, Bear said out loud "Won't be long before we get to the State line, BJ."

BJ sat up straight in the seat with a shocked look on his face. "Wow, I must have nodded off."

"Easy to do, I used to have this buddy of mine that would make runs with me that as soon as we got rolling, within five minutes would fall fast asleep. Shoot…old Shaun would sleep five or six hours then wake up, ask me where we were, and when was the next pit stop cause he had to go. Then he would take over and drive for hours. Worked out real good that way" said Bear.

"Speaking of a pit stop, when is the next one?" asked BJ.

"State line is just a few miles up ahead, rest stops on both sides, which state do you want to go in to?" asked Bear.

"Never been in Oklahoma" said BJ.

A few more minutes passed by when Bear exclaimed "Here comes the Red River, Texas State line!"

BJ looked out at the valley that lay before him, and the position of the sun laying low in the western sky made everything have a red glow to it. "I can see how the song "Red River Valley" was inspired, this is really beautiful."

As the pair passed over the bridge, BJ looked down into the water, and sure enough, the river was red. "How come the water is red?"

"Comes from the red clay along its banks" answered Bear.

"Rest stops just ahead, welcome to Oklahoma," Bear said as he looked over at BJ and nodded his head slightly.

As the pair reached the other side of the bridge, BJ spotted the sign that read "Oklahoma State Line" and thought to himself "still have two more to cross, hope they go faster than Texas did." Then he spotted another sign that read "Visitors' Center One Mile."

"The Visitors' Center, is that the rest stop?" he asked hopefully.

With a chuckle in his voice Bear answered "You bet it is, little buddy."

Bear hardly had the air brakes set before BJ had the door open and was climbing down the steps to the ground. Bear was just opening his door when BJ came running around the front of the rig and started heading towards the sidewalk to the restroom.

"Whoa, little buddy, slow down, you don't want to go in there alone, sometimes there are some seedy people hanging around these rest stops" exclaimed Bear.

"Oklahoma's that bad?" asked BJ.

"No, no...I mean all rest stops around the country," answered Bear as he hurried to catch up with BJ who was still walking at a rapid pace.

Coming out of the restroom BJ asked Bear "Is that the State map?" pointing at a map on a stand.

Looking in the direction BJ was pointing, he answered "Yeah, that's the state map, they have them at all rest stops. Tells you where you are in the State."

"Mind if I look at it for a minute?" asked BJ.

"No, go on and look at it, but don't take too long, I'll check my rig over while your looking" said Bear

BJ walked up to the map and noticed a big red star at the bottom of the map with a red arrow pointing to it. Printed on the arrow in black letters were the words "You are here." BJ's heart sank as he looked closer at the map and saw that Pauls Valley was only a short distance away from the star. He also noticed it was about one fourth of the way across the state. He made a mental map of Oklahoma with Pauls Valley at one quarter, Oklahoma City at one half, Perry at three quarters, and Blackwell as almost into Kansas. Walking back towards the rig he watched as Bear walked by all the tires and was hitting them with a wooden club.

"What are you doing that for?" asked BJ as he got closer to the rig.

"Just checking the tires, you ready to roll, little buddy?" asked Bear.

"You bet!" answered BJ.

As BJ walked around the front of the rig, a smile came across his face as he thought how he liked Bear calling him "little buddy."

A few minutes had passed as well as a few more miles up the freeway, when Bear looked over at BJ and said "Sure are being awfully quiet, little buddy."

BJ turned from looking out the window, and looking at Bear said "Oh, its just that I noticed we don't have that much further to go until we get to Pauls Valley, according to that map back at the rest stop" answered BJ.

"Probably another fifty miles or so…why?" asked Bear

"Nothing really…just that I really have enjoyed riding with you and hate to see it come to an end" answered BJ.

Bear glanced over at BJ who had turned back to look out the window, and a little smile came to his lips. As Bear looked back out the windshield he swallowed hard and thought "Yeah me too, little buddy."

Rolling along in silence, both lost in their own thoughts, the miles grew fewer and fewer until they would have to part. BJ was thinking of his mom and dad and wishing they were still here and wondering at the same time what his Uncle Bob's reaction was going to be. If he was even going to have a place to stay. Bear's mind was in a different place thinking how he could help his little buddy.

"That will work!" Bear said loudly all of a sudden causing BJ to jump slightly.

"What will work?" asked BJ.

"I just figured how I can help you a little more" said Bear with a big smile on his face.

"You've already done quite a lot, and I appreciate…"

"Nonsense," said Bear, cutting BJ off in mid-sentence, "You have no idea what you have done for me, little buddy. You have no idea how long I have built walls up around me so I wouldn't be hurt by other people. You have shown me that there is still some good in this world, and how helping someone in need is the greatest gift we can give. Little buddy, I haven't felt this good in years."

"Well I'm glad I helped, even though I don't know what I did. I know I'm going to miss you" said BJ.

"Yeah, I'm going to miss you, too. Tell you what, write your name and address on this piece of paper" Bear said as he handed the paper to BJ.

"I don't know the address where I will be staying" said BJ, as he wrote his name on the paper. Then, as an after thought,

"Truer words were never spoken, I may not even have a place to live."

"How about the name of the town?" asked Bear

"Well, yeah, I know that" said BJ as he wrote "Burwell, Nebraska."

Handing the paper back, Bear read out loud "Burwell...never know when I might be passing through there and need to see a friend," and gave BJ a wink.

"So, what did you figure out?" asked BJ.

"Oh yeah, I have this friend in Pauls Valley who runs a little restaurant called the Junction Cafe. All the truckers stop there, maybe she can hook you up with somebody heading further north" answered Bear.

"That would be extremely cool" said BJ as the pair crested another hill and saw a sign that read "Pauls Valley 5 miles."

Chapter Twenty-Six

The headlights of the rig reflected off the sign that read "Pauls Valley City Limits' and Bear started shifting down and put his right turn signal on and exited the highway. Pulling to the stop sign he turned left and passed under the overpass and said "There it is."

BJ looked up on the right side of the road and saw a large white sign with purple letters that read "Junction Cafe", written below was "Orders to go." As the rig pulled up and parked just off the pavement parallel with the street, Bear said "Make sure you get everything."

Bear walked around the front of the rig and was waiting for BJ to climb down when he said "Why don't you just leave everything up in there until we get through eating, maybe we can just transfer your things to another truck if we are lucky." Looking around the empty parking lot Bear thought to himself "Definitely going to take some of that."

A waitress waiting on one of the three outside tables on the porch that ran the length of the front of the cafe spotted Bear standing by his rig and quickly walked back inside to inform the other waitress that was new that one of the meanest customers she would ever wait on was coming in.

Walking up to the cafe BJ noticed in what light there was coming from the sign that this place wasn't painted a regular color. Looking up at Bear, BJ asked "What color is that?"

Bear smiled and answered "It's grey with purple trim, food's good, though."

The pair climbed the wooden steps, crossed the wooden porch and came to a pair of screen doors of which BJ pushed on the one to the right which didn't budge, then tried the one on the left, same thing. Bear reached around him and grabbed the small metal handle and pulled the left door open. "Everybody has a problem with those doors" said Bear with a chuckle.

"Well, every place I have been, it's always the door on the right and it opens in, not out" said BJ.

Walking through the door BJ was reminded of his dream, or whatever it was. The floor was wooden with the paths of many people worn into it. Looking around he realized he had never been in any place like this.

A young girl, probably high school age, finished serving one of the two tables occupied, walked up to the pair and said "You can sit anywhere you want. These two tables are non-smoking" she said, pointing to the tables along the wall right by the door they had just walked through.

"Thank you," said Bear.

"Yeah, thanks," said BJ with a big smile.

BJ followed Bear across the small room to a table by the back wall. On their way, Bear saw the man sitting with his family look up at him and nodded his head. Bear just nodded back at him. Sitting down BJ asked, "What was that about?"

We were just saying hello to each other. It is kind of like "How ya doin." Just a common courtesy," answered Bear.

The young waitress walked back behind a glass enclosed counter to where the other waitress was pouring a glass of iced tea for one of her customers. Turning from pouring the tea, she saw that Bear was sitting down in one of her sections.

"Why did you tell him to sit there?" asked the young waitress.

"I just told him the same thing we tell everybody," answered the young girl.

"What did he say when you told him? Where's Gina's station, I want to hassle her?" asked Gina.

"He just said thank you," answered Tiffany.

"He said thank you. He has never been thankful for anything in his life. Do me a favor and take their drink orders while I carry this tea outside, then I'll take over," Gina said.

"That's alright, I will wait on them. Should be good experience," Tiffany said.

"It will be a good experience, alright, thanks," said Gina. Handing menus to the two of them, Tiffany asked, "What can I get you guys to drink?" "Give me a cup of coffee and whatever he wants," said Bear looking over at BJ who was smiling from ear to ear. "Do you have Dr. Pepper?" stammered BJ.

"Coffee and a Dr. Pepper coming right up," Tiffany said with a smile and walked away. BJ turned and watched her as she walked away. Turning back toward Bear, he saw a big smile on Bear's face. "What?" asked BJ.

"Down boy. She is too old for you," said Bear with a chuckle in his voice.

Returning with their drinks, Tiffany asked, "Have you guys decided what you would like?"

Looking over at BJ, who was sitting as tall as he could, Bear just smiled and said, "Give me the ham steak, four eggs over medium, and biscuits if you have them." BJ wanting to look older and realizing he hadn't even looked at the menu, just said, "Make that the same for me," and turned bright red.

As Tiffany started to walk away, Bear asked, "Is Christine around?" "Yeah, she's in the office. Want me to get her?"

"No, I'll talk to her later, thanks," said Bear.

Waiting on their food, BJ looked around the room and was amazed at all the stuff hanging on the walls and from the beams across the ceilings. Then, he noticed the chairs.

"Why are all the chairs different?" he asked Bear.

"I asked Chris the same thing once. She said she saw it on some show, and thought it was unique. Actually, I think it's something you always will remember about the place," answered Bear.

When their food was brought to them, Tiffany simply said, "Enjoy." BJ now too embarrassed to even look up at her was dumbstruck at the size of the plate that was set before him. Actually, it was a platter with a whole ham steak about half an inch thick, four eggs and fried sliced potatoes, and two of the biggest biscuits he had ever seen in his life on a separate plate. Looking up from his plate and across the table to Bear, he said, "I guess I should have listened to what you ordered. I don't know if I can eat all of this."

With a big smile on his face Bear replied, "You had other things on our mind. Just enjoy as much as you can. Knowing Chris, she probably has an old dog that will enjoy what you don't finish."

The pair sat in silence as they ate their supper, both knowing that as they finished, it wouldn't be long before they would have to say goodbye and head out their separate ways. Wiping up the last of the egg yolk with the last part of his biscuit, Bear said just above a whisper, "You never know."

Looking up from a half finished plate, BJ asked, "What do you never know?"

Slightly startled, Bear replied, "Oh I was just thinking out loud. It's nothing." "Do you know where the restrooms are?" asked BJ.

"Yeah, right through that opening up there by the front door, next to the Juke box," said Bear pointing to the end of the room.

"You had all you want?" asked Bear nodding toward BJ's plate.

"Definitely, sorry I couldn't finish it," BJ answered.

"That's alright, maybe they can make you a couple of ham sandwiches out of what is left. You might need it later on," suggested Bear.

While BJ was in the restroom, Chris came out of her office that was also back in that opening beside the restrooms. She was carrying her coffee cup, heading toward the kitchen that was behind the glass counter when she looked and spotted Bear sitting, looking down at his empty plate. Setting her cup on the counter, she walked up to Bear, undetected.

"It's been a long time Bear," she said softly. Looking up from where he was sitting Bear smiled and said, "Hello Chris," then he stood up and gave her a gentle hug, which she returned.

Moving over and sitting back down in the chair next to the wall, he offered Chris the chair he had been occupying.

Sitting next to him, Chris noticed the half finished plate across the table and asked, "Your friend didn't like the food?"

"You will understand when you see him," answered Bear with a smile. "It's been a long time, what have you been up to?" asked Chris, noticing the gleam in Bear's eyes.

"Traveling the east coast mostly. Wasn't even supposed to be on this run, but the company called when another driver couldn't make it, so here I am," answered Bear.

"Well, you are looking good. Haven't seen you look this happy in years," said Chris.

"Chris, I have a little favor to ask of you," said Bear.

"Whatever I can do for you," answered Chris.

About that time, BJ walked out of the restroom and headed toward the table. "Here comes the favor I need," said Bear.

Chris turned toward the direction of BJ and said, "Hi, my name's Chris" and extended her hand, which BJ took in his hand and shook.

"Robert Joseph Stephens, Maam. My friends call me BJ" said BJ.

"Well then, BJ it is," answered Chris.

BJ sat down in his seat and listened as Bear asked his favor.

"So, what's this favor you need?" asked Chris.

"Well, BJ and I hooked up down in Centerville, Texas. He's trying to get up to central Nebraska. I have a drop in Ada, Oklahoma. Then I am on up to Tulsa, then Joplin, Missouri. I was wondering if you knew anybody that was heading up to maybe Wichita, that he could catch a ride with?" asked Bear.

"Well, I can keep an eye out for him. I don't know of anybody right now, but I sure will help him" answered Chris.

"I knew I could count on you. Thank you," said Bear. "Thank you, Maam," said BJ.

"You sure are polite, little boy. Somebody brought you up right," said Chris.

Gina walked up about that time with a pot of coffee in her hand and asked, "Would you like some coffee, Bear?" When Bear looked up at her and said, "No thank you," she also saw a softness she had never seen in him.

"Well, I have to finish some stuff in the office," said Chris as she stood up.

"Yeah, I need to be getting on my way also," said Bear as he stood up. BJ stood up as the two passed by his seat heading for the cash register, and followed them. Seeing Bear reach for his wallet, Chris said, "It's on the house, and I don't want to hear any argument."

Bear turned to BJ and said, "Well, I guess you'd better come and get your belongings out of the truck."

Chris reached up and hugged Bear around the neck. Letting go, she said, "Don't make it so long next time."

Tiffany and Gina, standing behind the counter both said their goodbyes, and when Bear walked out the door, Tiffany turned to Gina and said, "'If that's the meanest customer I ever wait on, this job's going to be a piece of cake."

"Something, or someone, has touched his heart," was all Gina could say as the two went back to their different duties.

Bear and his little buddy walked slowly back to the rig, neither one of them in a hurry to say goodbye. Bear reached up and unlocked the passenger side door and opened it. BJ climbed up the steps to the cab and pulled out his backpack and blanket and handed them down to Bear. Retrieving his sign, BJ climbed back down from the rig.

"Well I guess that's everything," said BJ quietly.

"Not quite everything," said Bear as he climbed up in his rig and pulled a little blue teddy bear from out of the sleeper cab of the truck and handed it to BJ The bear was no bigger than BJ's palm. "What's this?" asked BJ as he looked down at it.

"Just something for you to remember me by," said Bear as he choked back the tears. BJ looked up at Bear and with tears in his own eyes, he said, "I don't need anything to remember you by. I will always remember you."

Bear squatted down a little and BJ wrapped his arms around Bear the best he could and they hugged goodbye.

Standing back up, Bear said, "I only say goodbye when it is permanent. So, to you I'll say, "See ya later." With that, Bear went around the other side of the rig, climbed in and drove away.

BJ stood in the parking lot and watched as the taillights grew dimmer and dimmer, and then were gone.

BJ felt what he thought was a tear on his cheek and wiped it away, only to find his cheek was dry.

Chapter Twenty-Seven

BJ picked up his backpack and blanket from the ground and turned toward the cafe. Seeing Chris standing on the porch waiting for him reminded him of his mom when she would wait for him on the nights he would leave Chipper's after dark. She would stand there making sure he was safe. The flood of tears he had been holding back rushed forward. The healing continues.

Seeing BJ standing out there in the dark and not knowing the history behind his pain, Chris only saw a young child lost in the dark. It set off the involuntary reflex that all mothers have. Chris rushed out into the darkness and held him while he cried.

After a few minutes the pair walked back up to the now vacant porch of the cafe and sat down at one of the tables.

The pair sat in silence a few moments, BJ sitting across from Chris with his elbows propped on his knees, and his head hanging down. He was looking at the little blue bear in his hands. Chris sat looking back and forth from BJ to the darkness.

The last two customers came out the front door saying goodnight to Chris with a "See ya later." Chris responded with a thank you.

Turning back to BJ, Chris said, "Well that's the last of them for today." BJ turned and watched the couple walk down the front steps, then looked over at Chris and asked, "Have you known Bear a long time?"

"Oh yes, Bear and I go way back. We went to school together. We even tried dating, but we were too good of friends for that to go anywhere," answered Chris.

"Really!" said BJ who had now sat up straight and turned toward Chris. As BJ put his hands up on the table, Chris spotted the little blue bear.

"Where'd you get that?" asked Chris nodding toward the bear. Holding the bear up, BJ replied, "Bear gave it to me just before he left. He said it was something to remember him by. Why?"

"Like I said, I have known Bear a long time, about seven, no I guess eight years now. Bear was out on a run when his wife and baby son were killed when their home caught fire. Bear came home and buried his family, which was all he had. He was an orphan and just lived with foster folks for a while before he met his wife. Been a trucker all his life. He would come back every now and then. When he met Elizabeth and got married, he was around more, but still had to do his job. After the funeral, he hardly ever came around. He just closed up somehow. He became mean, for a lack of a better description. Tonight is the first time I've seen the old Bear, the one I used to know, in a long time" explained Chris.

"That little bear used to hang from an elastic band in Bear's rig for years. He bought it for his son, and was going to give it to him, but it was too late," Chris paused.

"You must have really struck a cord with Bear."

"All I know is he was really mean when I first met him, then he changed," said BJ Chris smiled and said, "Whatever it was you did, broke the chains around his heart and set him free."

"I don't know if I did anything!" said BJ. "BJ, through your life, you will meet people. Some you will know all your life, some for years, and some for just hours, like Bear. These people will have an impact on you for the rest of your life. We don't know when or where we will meet them, but we never forget them. Just like Bear will never forget you," said Chris.

"I know one thing Bear taught me," said BJ.

"What's that?" asked Chris as she stood up.

"People aren't always what you think they are when you first meet them, you have to get to know them," answered BJ.

"So true, BJ, so true," said Chris as she turned and headed for the door. I have to start closing this place up and figure what I'm going to do with you for the night."

BJ barely heard her as he stared at the little bear and thought, "So that's where you did get your name. God please watch over him."

Chris followed Gina and Tiffany out the front door and bid them goodnight. Walking over to where BJ was sitting, she said, "Well, now what do I do with you, young man?"

Looking up to where Chris was standing, BJ said, "I'll be alright. Maybe I can just wait here for another trucker to come by."

"Nonsense. There won't be any more truckers by till the morning," she said as she pointed toward the sign out by the highway. "Once that sign is off, they all know I'm closed." "Well, if it is all the same to you, Miss Chris, maybe I could just sleep here on the porch till the morning," said BJ.

"Nonsense, I just couldn't…"

"Miss Chris, I don't want to be a bother to anybody, and who knows, a trucker could come by and I could be back on the road much sooner," said BJ cutting off Chris in mid-sentence.

"I promised Bear that I would take care of you," said Chris.

BJ turned away from looking at Chris and just stared out into the darkness.

"Okay, you win…you can sleep here, but promise me one thing!" said Chris. BJ turned back toward Chris. "Promise me you will be here in the morning. Not all the truckers are like Bear. He asked me to make sure I got you a ride with someone I knew. Will you do that for me?" asked Chris.

BJ smiled and said, "Sure. I promise I will wait, but if one doesn't come along early, I will have to set out on my own, okay?"

"That's fine," Chris said as she reached across the table and patted BJ on the arm. "I will see you in the morning."

BJ watched as Chris rose from her chair, walked across the porch and down the steps to her car. As she opened the door of her car, he hollered out, "Thank you."

Chris just raised her hand and waved, climbed into her car, backed out onto the road and drove away.

BJ sat there in the darkness for a moment thinking of the people he had met so far on his trip. He said a silent prayer for them all. In the only light there was coming from the light left on inside the kitchen, BJ rolled his blanket out on the floor by the wall along the backside of the porch. Rolled up in his blanket and using his backpack for his pillow, BJ fell asleep clutching the little blue bear to his chest.

Chapter Twenty-Eight

Chris arrived back at the cafe at her usual 6:00 AM, and as usual there were already a couple of rigs parked along the highway. She didn't recognize either one, and since they were both pointed south, it didn't matter. Walking up on the porch to open the front door, Chris glanced over at a lump on the floor and smiled. "God bless you, child," she thought to herself.

A couple of minutes later, after Chris had turned on the lights, she heard the door open and saw an old friend walk in.

"Well, hello Harvey. Didn't hear you pull up," she said as she thought, "What luck for BJ."

"Hello, Chris, didn't hear me cause I was parked already," said Harvey. Chris walked over to where Harvey sat down and said, "Coffee will be ready in a minute. You driving for someone else now?"

"Yeah, got tired of all those east coast runs," Harvey answered.

Chris looked out into the dawning light and still only seeing two rigs said, "Heading south?"

"Yes Maam, Rio Grande Valley," answered Harvey.

"Know anybody heading north?" asked Chris.

"This got anything to do with that lump over there on the porch?" asked Harvey. Chris told Harvey about BJ and her promise to Bear. "Just a kid trying to get up to Nebraska. He caught a ride with Bear up to here, and I promised Bear I would keep an eye out for someone I trusted to give him a ride further up north. He is a really good kid."

"Well, the only one me and you know that's heading up north is 'Cowboy'. I talked to him a little while ago. He rolled out of Shreveport and is heading to Wichita. He ought to be here in a couple of hours," stated Harvey.

"Thank you Harvey. Let me get you a cup of coffee. You want eggs and ham?" Chris asked.

"Yes, also you might want to wake that boy up before Bartow gets here. Sure enough he will pick that boy up for vagrancy," said Harvey.

Chris hadn't even thought of Bartow, the County Sheriff. Sure as the day was light, he would pick up BJ

Handing the cup of coffee to Harvey, Chris looked at the clock on the wall. Noting the time was 6:20 meant she only had a few minutes to get BJ up and inside. Rushing out onto the porch, she, reached and shook BJ awake. "BJ...BJ, you have to get up!"

BJ sat up groggily looking around, trying to get is bearings, when he heard, "BJ you have to get inside right now!

BJ jumped up and looked at Chris and asked just above a whisper, "What's wrong?" "I will explain as soon as we go inside. Grab your things!" Chris said, as she bent over and scooped up BJ's backpack.

BJ slowly bent over and picked up his ball cap and put it on over his mussed hair. Bending slowly over again to get his blanket, Chris bent over and grabbed a corner of the blanket and snatched it to herself in a wad and said, "Quick, let's get inside."

BJ followed Chris inside her office and she explained to BJ about Bartow.

"Well, what do I do?" asked BJ.

"First, you go into the bathroom and freshen up. Then, you come out and come into the kitchen. We will figure something out from there," said Chris.

BJ had no sooner locked the restroom door, and Chris had returned to the kitchen, when Bartow came in through the front door.

"How ya doing?" said Bartow, seeing Harvey sitting there.

"Just fine, Bartow. How are you?" said Harvey.

Bartow didn't answer which was fine with Harvey. He just sat down at the same table, in the same chair, with his back to the wall as he had been doing for the past three years plus. And, he always came in between 6:25 and 6:30 A.M.

Chris came out of the kitchen with a cup of coffee and sat it down on Bartow's table.

"Good morning, Bartow." Same as usual, I suppose," said Chris.

"Right as rain," answered Bartow.

Chris returned to the kitchen and proceeded to cook the breakfasts that were ordered. BJ had done the best he could with his hair, and had washed his face when he heard a knock on the bathroom door. "Just a second," BJ said. BJ straightened his ball cap and opened the door. There stood Bartow in the small area between the bathroom and the opening into the dining area.

"Excuse me," BJ said as he squeezed between Bartow and the wall.

"Excuse me," Bartow said as he inhaled to let BJ by.

BJ hurried into the kitchen and asked Chris, "What should I do?"

"Just pretend that you are my cousin's boy here to visit. Leave the rest to me. Start washing these plates, said Chris as she put a couple of clean plates in the sink.

Bartow returned to his table about the same time Chris came out with his and Harvey's breakfasts. Chris sat Bartow's down first, as he was closer to the kitchen. Then she proceeded on to Harvey's table. Walking back toward the kitchen Chris asked Bartow, "Will you need anything else?"

"Yeah, you can bring me some more coffee when you get a chance," answered Bartow. He then added, "Where's that boy that was in the restroom?"

"He's in the kitchen. That's my cousin Thelma's boy from down in Houston. He is going to stay with me for a week so she and her husband can go on a second honeymoon. Don't you think that's the most precious thing?" answered Chris.

"Yeah, that's nice," answered Bartow, not impressed.

"Yeah, he just wanted to come up and help me. You know, he's all excited about something new. But I am sure come tomorrow morning he will just sleep like most teenagers. Probably won't even see him around any…"

"Chris, don't you know I am on a time schedule? I don't have time to chat with you, and I really don't care about your family tree," snapped Bartow.

"Well, excuse me," said Chris as she looked over at Harvey who winked back at her.

Chris was in the kitchen when she heard a rustle of a chair. Walking out to the cash register, she saw Bartow standing by the front door. "We'll see you tomorrow, Bartow. You be careful." The door no sooner shut, when Chris and Harvey both started laughing about pulling one over on Bartow. Then all of a sudden, the door opened back up and Bartow was standing in the door.

"I found this out here on the porch. Some kid must have lost it," said Bartow, as be placed the little blue bear on the table right next to the door.

I'll see it is returned to its rightful owner, thanks," said Chris, as Bartow closed the door behind him.

Harvey walked up to the counter at about the same time BJ peeked around the door to the kitchen. Chris, standing by the cash register, said "Harvey, yours is on the house, too. Just do me one favor in return."

"Well, thanks. What do you want me to do'" asked Harvey.

"You get on that CB and get a hold of 'Cowboy' and make sure he comes by here. Tell him I got a load for him to haul!" said Chris.

"Sure thing, Chris. Consider it done. See ya," said Harvey as he walked toward the front door.

"You be careful out there, bye," said Chris as Harvey closed the door behind him.

A little over an hour passed. BJ had eaten his breakfast and insisted on washing dishes for his meal. Chris was serving a couple of local people when she heard the sound of a big rig stopping out front. Looking out the front window, she saw the tallest, skinniest cowboy you have ever seen walk out from around the front of his rig and a big smile appeared on her face. Cowboy was here.

Chris went out on the front porch and met Cowboy as he reached the steps. Still two steps down from the top, she reached for him and they gave each other a long hug.

Releasing each other, Cowboy said, "When you going to let me make an honest woman of you?"

"When you stop running the roads and settle down. How ya doing, Cowboy?" said Chris with a big smile. "Just fine. Heard you need a favor. Harvey called me and said you need a load hauled," answered Cowboy.

"Yeah, he's inside," said Chris.

"He?" said Cowboy, as they passed through the door.

Standing inside the door, Chris told Cowboy everything she knew about BJ About how Bear had helped him and her promise to Bear. Cowboy agreed to do what he could to help.

Walking into the kitchen, the pair found BJ up to his elbows in dish suds. BJ turned as the pair walked in and smiled. "Tell me this is my ride, and I am relieved of kitchen duty," said BJ.

"BJ, this is a very old friend of mine, everybody calls him Cowboy," said Chris. BJ quickly grabbed a dishtowel and dried his hands. Laying the towel back down on the counter, he turned and offered his hand to Cowboy. Cowboy's hand completely covered BJ's small hand as they shook. "Bill Stephens Jr., my friends call me BJ," said BJ.

"Shaun Michael Mcgurdy, but everybody calls me Cowboy," said Cowboy with a smile. "I hate to sound pushy, but I think it would be a good idea if you guys got on the road. You never know when Bartow might come snooping around," said Chris.

"Yeah, you are right. I need to get on the way anyway. I am already behind schedule as it is," said Cowboy.

"You make sure to get all your things, BJ," said Chris.

BJ moved around the pair standing there and went to where his backpack and blanket were laying. As he was rolling up his blanket, he heard Chris say, "You take good care of him. He's a good kid."

"You can count on it, Chris," answered Cowboy as he reached over and hugged her. As the three of them walked out of the kitchen, Chris asked, "Would you like a cup of coffee to go?"

"No thanks, I have a full thermos in the rig. BJ might want something though," said Cowboy.

"No offense, Miss Chris, but the only thing I want is to get on the road," said BJ. "Okay, Cowboy you go out first and make sure the coast is clear. If Bartow pulled up and saw BJ climbing into your rig, he might make a big deal about it, said Chris.

"Okay," said Cowboy as the three of them walked to the front door. Stopping inside the door as Cowboy walked out to his rig, BJ turned and picked up the little blue bear off the table where Bartow had set it down, and put it in his backpack. Turning toward Chris, BJ said, "I want to thank you for all you have done."

Bending over and giving BJ a hug, Chris said, "The pleasure was all mine, BJ, I hope you find what you are looking for. Now get going."

As BJ reached Cowboy's rig, he turned and saw Chris standing on the porch. As he raised his hand and waved goodbye, Chris hollered, "You come back and see me sometime!"

As BJ stood on the top step of the rig with a big smile on his face, he hollered back, "I will, I promise."

Chapter Twenty-Nine

As Cowboy pulled the rig up to the stop light at the intersection with I-35, BJ spotted a sign that read "Oklahoma City 55." As Cowboy started pulling through the green light BJ asked "Does that mean we are only fifty-five miles from Oklahoma City?"

"That it does" answered Cowboy as he came out from under the I-35 overpass and turned left onto the on-ramp.

"So, how far will I be riding with you?" asked BJ.

"Well, I have a load to drop off in Salina, Kansas then I'm Eastbound from there. Chris said you were headed to Nebraska, so I guess we'll be together till Salina, if that's alright' with you." answered Cowboy.

"Is Salina very far into Kansas?" asked BJ.

"Probably two thirds of the way through Kansas, about seventy-five miles north of Wichita" answered Cowboy.

"Wichita Kansas, that is one of the big cowboy towns of the old west isn't it?" asked BJ.

"Well, yeah it was, it's where all the cattle drives out of Texas ended up, at least most of them" explained Cowboy.

While the pair rolled North on 35, Gracie was sitting on the top step of Buck's front porch drinking a cup of coffee she had just made. Turk had been laying beside her when all of a sudden he jumped up and turned toward the front door just as Buck opened it. Turk walked slowly over to the front door with his tail wagging and his head hanging slightly. As the door closed behind him Buck reached down with his free hand and gave Turk a pat on the head and a little scratch behind the ear and said "Good morning, buddy." Satisfied, Turk followed Buck as he walked across the porch and sat down next to Gracie.

"Good morning, baby" said Buck.

"Good morning, I hope I didn't wake you, I tried to be quite" answered Gracie.

"No, no you didn't wake me, actually I hardly slept" said Buck.

"Yeah I know, you tossed and turned and kept talking in your sleep" said Gracie.

"What was I talking about?" asked Buck

"Nothing that made much sense, only thing I could really make out was something about Bones picking up, or picking Cotton, or something like that. Then you said something about walking, and you did mention Gunter. I am so sorry you have those nightmares. If there is anything I can ever do, you just ask, okay?" said Gracie

"I don't remember any nightmares, in fact the only thing I can remember is a little boy who was just walking along looking at the dust he was kicking up with his feet. I have no idea what that is supposed to mean" said Buck.

"Bill called me, I guess, the same day he was…he died. He was trying to get in touch with you, said he wanted to come up and try to patch things up between you guys. He told me to tell you he loved you and that too much water had passed under the bridge. He was going to come up before the end of summer." Gracie barely got the last words out before her voice started cracking.

"Yeah I was thinking a lot about him lately, time seems to slip by so quickly, days turn into years before you know it. Next thing you know your sitting and thinking how you wish you had done it different." Buck said

"It's like they say "There is no time like the present" said Gracie

The pair sat in silence for a few moments watching an eagle fly in circles over the cornfields. A pickup truck drove by the front of Buck's place, and someone driving the truck waved and the pair waved back.

Buck watched as the truck drove out of sight and then said "I think I'm going to drive into Ord (the County seat) and see the Sheriff, find out what I can about Bill."

"Want some company?" asked Gracie

"Sure...Gracie, you said there was no time like the present, you know I have loved you a long time" said Buck

"Well yes I have known that, and I love you too" said Gracie as she watched Buck stand up and turn towards her and then get down on one knee.

"Gracie...Will you marry me?" asked Buck

"OH!!...Yes, yes...Yes!" exclaimed Gracie as she stood up from her seat on the steps and dove into Buck's waiting arms and kissed him.

"I love you so much, baby" said Buck

"And I love you so much" said Gracie as she hugged him tightly to her body.

Separating, Buck looked at Gracie and said "Well, baby, you don't have to cry over it."

"These are tears of joy. I have waited so long to hear those words" said Gracie, as she placed her head on his shoulder and embraced the man she has loved so long.

"While we are in Ord we can go and find you an engagement ring. I want to do this right" said Buck.

"Not too long of an engagement, I hope" exclaimed Gracie

"No, just long enough to let people know how much I love you" said Buck.

"Let me freshen up a little and get my purse and I'll be ready," Gracie said and kissed Buck and turned to leave. At the top of the steps she turned back towards Buck and said "I love you, Bob Stephens," and then she turned and went through the front door.

Chapter Thirty

The pair pulled out of Buck's place, leaving Turk behind, as it could turn out to be a long day. They passed by Gracie's and onto the highway and turned right heading east toward Burwell. As they passed to the south of Burwell on the highway, Gracie said "If you don't mind, I would like to get our rings at Stewart's Jewelers."

Glancing out the window to his left at the water tower in Burwell and remembering Stewart's as the place his parents had gone to get their rings, and also where he and Bill had gotten their high school senior rings, Buck replied "That is exactly where I figured we would go" and smiled at his bride to be.

There was only small talk as the pair headed south on the Highway to Ord, both kind of lost in their own thoughts. When they passed by Elyria, a town with a population of 60 Gracie broke the silence when she asked "Have you figured out who the little boy is?"

"I haven't really thought a lot about it" answered Buck

"It's the same one that the old black man said to take care of, I think" replied Gracie.

Buck stared into Gracie's eyes trying to find the answer, "Who?" asked Buck

"BJ, Bill's son, your nephew!" exclaimed Gracie.

Buck recoiled as if he had been slapped in the face. "Me!!!...I can't be taking care of him, I can hardly take care of me!"

"You, or should I now say we, are all he has in this world, baby!" said Gracie

"Your right...I know all too well what it's like to be alone" then he looked over at Gracie and said "But never again."

Gracie leaned over in the truck and kissed Buck on the cheek "You are so special" she said.

They drove on in silence as the cornfields passed by like soldiers at attention. Driving into Ord, a town rarely visited by Buck, he said "Nothing's changed around here, I see."

"Baby, when was the last time you saw anything change anywhere around here. Been the same since we were kids." said Gracie.

"That's the truth" said Buck as he pulled into the angle parking spot in front of the Sheriff's Department.

Walking into the Sheriff's Department Gracie spotted Ty Jergens, an old friend of hers she had dated a couple of times in the far distant past.

"Well, hello Deputy Jergens" said Gracie.

Looking up from his desk Ty just smiled and said as he rose to his feet "Well, hello Gracie, what brings you into the big town?"

"We have some business with the Sheriff. Is he in?" asked Gracie.

Walking up to the partition that separated the desks from the waiting area, Ty answered "Well, no, he had to go into Omaha on some business, can I help you?"

"Well, we hope so. Ty Jergens, this is Bob Stephens, my fiancé" said Gracie

Ty extended his hand, and as the two shook, Ty said "Well congratulations to the both of you" and with a slight pause continued "What can I do to help you two?"

"My brother, Bill, was killed a couple of weeks ago. I just got back in town yesterday and I would like to see if I could find out any details. I really don't know how to pursue this and I need your help." said Buck

"Okay…where did this take place?" asked Ty

"Houston, Texas" answered Buck.

"When?" asked Ty

Buck looked over at Gracie who said "A little over two weeks."

"What would you like me to do?" asked Ty

"I thought you had some kind of procedure you followed to check up on these kinds of things" asked Buck

"Well, I can call Houston, I guess…tell you what, let me call Sheriff Scott and ask him if there is some kind procedure to follow. Honestly I have never come across anything like this" said Ty

"Us either" said Buck with an edge of agitation in his voice.

"Why don't you guys sit down there and give me a couple of minutes" said Ty pointing to some chairs along the wall by the front door.

Ty walked back to his desk and got on the phone, and after a few minutes, amid a lot of "Yes' and okays," he got off the phone and walked back to the partition and opened the half door and said "You two want to come in here."

Buck and Gracie walked through the little door and followed Ty to his desk and sat down in front of the desk.

"Okay, this is what we have to do, I will call Houston and find out who handled the case. It could be the City, County Sheriff or Highway Patrol. After I find that, out you, Mr. Stephens, will have to get on the phone and verify who you are to whichever department is handling the case." said Ty

"Okay let's get started" said Buck in a much calmer voice.

"I guess the best place to start would be the City guys," said Ty as he dialed Information. The second call to Harris County Sheriff's Department proved to be the one they needed.

After Buck verified who he was, he was put on hold to wait for a detective to get off another line. After a few minutes of waiting, Gracie could see the aggravation growing on Bucks face.

"Give them a little time, Honey, they are a big town, probably very busy, okay?" Gracie stated.

"Yeah, your right" answered Buck

Another minute passed by, then a voice on the other end said "Detective Hawley, how can I help you?"

"Yes, Sir, I am trying to find out about my brother. He was killed a little over two weeks ago, and I'm…

"What is your brother's name, please?" asked the Detective.

"Bill Stephens" answered Buck.

"I am going to put you on hold, please wait" said the detective.

"They put me on hold again" said Buck as he rested his head in his left hand and held the phone to his ear with his right.

After what seemed like an eternity the Detective came back on the phone.

"Okay, Mr. Stephens, how can I help you?"

"Well, I guess first of all I would like to know how my Brother died and where" said Buck.

"As best we can tell, your brother was involved in a new type of crime. He was shot and killed while waiting for a red light to change. His car was stolen, and we still haven't found it.

"Are you telling me my brother was killed for his car?" asked Buck

"Yes sir, we believe that to be true. It is what we call 'car jacking', a new crime that we are starting to see a lot of around here. They steal the car and either strip them for the parts or sell them across the border into Mexico. Finding the perpetrator is almost impossible as there are no finger prints and no witnesses. We did contact a co-worker of your brother's, and they had been working until early in the morning. He was on his way home when it happened. We are still working on the case, and if we come up with anything, how can we get in touch with you, Mr. Stephens?" asked the detective.

"They want somehow to get in touch with me if they find anything out, can I give them this number?" Buck asked Ty.

"Sure, definitely" answered Ty

"Ask them about BJ!" said Gracie

Buck gave the detective the number to the Sheriff's Department and then asked, "My brother had a son, can you tell me how I can find him?"

"How old is this boy?" asked the detective

"Thirteen, I think" answered Buck

"I would imagine he's with his mother" answered the detective

"His mother has been dead for a couple of years now!" said Buck angrily

"I'm sorry, I didn't know. In that case I will transfer you over to C.P.S., and they should be able to help you" said the detective

"C.P.S., what's that?" asked Buck

"Child Protective Services, they take care of children under circumstances like this. I am sorry if I sound so callous, but we have so many cases a day like this. I wish you the best of luck, and if it's any help, just know that this guy that did this to your brother will be caught. If I can be of any help, please don't hesitate to call. Please stay on the line and I will transfer you." said the detective.

Buck looked over at Gracie and said "Someone killed him for his car and they don't have any clues."

"For his car, what is this world coming to, what did they say about BJ?" asked Gracie.

"They have me on hold while they are transferring me again to something called Child Protective Services" said Buck

"Sorry to hear all this, Bob, give me a small town any day" said Ty

"Boy, you ain't never lied about that" said Buck

"I totally agree" said Gracie

About that time a woman's voice came on the other end of the line.

"Child Protective Services, how can I help you?"

"Yes, Maam, I am trying to locate my nephew" said Buck

"Your name and the child's name, please?"

"Bob Stephens, and my nephew is Bill Stephens Jr., everybody calls him BJ for short." Buck answered.

"One moment, please, while I verify this."

Buck looked at Gracie and Ty "They got me on hold again, everybody treats this like its just some kind of business, there is no feeling at all." said Buck

"They probably see so much of this that they are just numbers to them" said Gracie.

"Sir" came the voice on the phone.

"Yes, Maam?" answered Buck

"As far as I can tell, your nephew was supposed to have been picked up this morning, but when the officer went by where he was staying, he could not be found."

"So how do I find him!" said Buck loudly

"Sir, you can lower your tone of voice, or I will have to end this conversation." "The place he was supposed to be at, is there a number I can call, please?" said Buck in a calmer voice.

"That's better...it is a private residence. The procedure is you give me a number for them to get in contact with you, that way we protect their privacy."

"Okay, you can give them 555-988-9001, and we will be waiting for the call" said Buck

"Also, I need to inform you that your nephew is considered a runaway, and also, according to my files the number you gave me is out of State. If your nephew shows up there, please contact us so we can send paperwork to you and the State of Nebraska."

"Yes, Maam, we will contact you." said Buck as he hung the phone up.

"So what's going on?" asked Gracie

"I had to give them your number so they can call the place BJ was staying at. I don't really understand everything that's going on. Apparently after Bill was killed, BJ must have been staying with friends. For some reason this CPS outfit was going to pick him, up but he wasn't there. Maybe these other people can enlighten us later." answered Buck.

"So I guess we ought to head back to my house and wait for their call?" asked Gracie.

"I think we could probably stop in Burwell on our way home" said Buck.

They both thanked Ty for his help and walked outside. On the way to the truck Gracie said to buck "I wonder where he is."

"Wherever he is, I just have a feeling he is in good hands, at least I hope he is" said Buck.

At the same time Gracie and Buck were driving back towards Burwell, BJ and his new friend were nearing the exit to Blackwell, Oklahoma.

"Well, this is the last exit except for the State line exit in Oklahoma" said Cowboy.

"So next stop is somewhere in Kansas, right?" asked BJ.

"There's a truck stop about thirty miles on the other side of the line, a town called Wellington, getting hungry?" asked Cowboy

"How far is that from here?" asked BJ.

"Somewhere around fifty miles, forty to forty-five minutes, I figure" answered Cowboy

"Yeah, I figure I will be hungry by then." A resounding growl from BJ's stomach seemed to verify this, and they both laughed.

Looking out the window, BJ started counting the telephone poles as they passed by and realized that each one they passed was taking him closer to a destination he was unsure of and further from what he had been so sure of. Tears welled up in his eyes as an accumulation of fear of the unknown future, and regret from the past, became so vivid.

Cowboy glanced over at BJ just about the time BJ wiped the tears from his cheeks as he looked out the side window, and Cowboy thought "I can sure see now what happened to Bear and Chris, this little fella will steal your heart" and then he started thinking of his own children. The pair rode on with nothing but the sound of the engine to accompany their thoughts.

BJ looked out the front window just in time to see a large green sign shaped like the State of Kansas with "Welcome to Kansas" written in white letters on it. There was no river this time marking the boundary, and BJ exclaimed "Wow I would have missed that, except for the sign!"

Cowboy kind of jerked at BJ's exuberant outburst and chuckled "Well not all States have a definite border like a river."

BJ was looking out the side window behind them into Oklahoma and beside them at Kansas, and he turned towards Cowboy and asked "Do you think there might be people who have houses half in Oklahoma and half in Kansas since there is no river?"

Cowboy had to laugh out loud at this.

Just as serious as can be, BJ said "Well it could happen!"

After Cowboy regained his composure, he said "Oh boy...I needed that" and broke out laughing again.

BJ broke into a big grin and said "What?"

Oh...I can just see a house with a wall down the middle of it, one side Kansas State fans and the other side OU fans, and the battles that would go on during football season" Cowboy said between chuckles.

Then BJ, caught up in the contagious laughter, said "Yeah...and the chicken coop would be half white chickens and half red chickens."

"They would have to have two front doors" exclaimed Cowboy, and burst out laughing as he wiped the tears from laughing from his own cheeks.

The two went down the highway caught up laughing contagiously, even just looking at the other one would cause them to burst out laughing. Finally able to have some composure, Cowboy said "Thanks I needed that."

"Yeah, me too" said BJ.

"Look! there's the sign for Wellington" said BJ.

"Chow time" said Cowboy

As Cowboy was pulling into the truck stop in Wellington, Buck and Gracie were pulling up in front of Stewart's Jewelers in Burwell.

Gracie reached for Bucks hand and squeezed it hard as they sat in the truck "I am so nervous!"

"To tell you the truth, I have butterflies, too" said Buck and then he leaned over and gave her a gentle kiss on the cheek.

Gracie turned, and with tears of joy in her eyes, she said "I have loved you for so long."

They leaned into each other and as soft as angels wings, their lips met. Standing by the front door they both looked at each other with faces all aglow and kissed each other gently again "You have no idea how many times I have dreamed of this exact moment, of standing here with you at this exact spot, I don't want it to ever end" said Gracie

"I have loved you for as long as I can remember. I think I started loving you from that first day on the pond. I know my love for you has grown through the years. I will love you forever and a day" said Buck, and then he turned and opened the door for his bride to be.

As the pair walked in, Joe Stewart, a man in his late sixties, was just coming out of a door behind the counter. Noticing the pair he had known since they were little kids, he said "Well I'll be, the last time I saw you two in here together was when you were trick-or-treating as kids. What can I do for you, not that I don't have an idea, the way you are both beaming."

"Bobby asked me to marry him!" Gracie almost shrieked.

"Well, congratulations to the both of you" said Joe

"Thank you, Mr. Stewart" said Buck

"Thank you, Joe" said Gracie

"You know, I was standing behind this very same counter when I sold both of your parents their wedding rings" said Joe.

"Well, we want to pick out an engagement ring first, and put our wedding rings on hold, or whatever you call it, so no one else can buy them, if that's alright with you" said Buck

"Whatever you want is fine with me, take your time and look them over" Joe said with a look on his face like the cat that ate the Canary.

"What is that look about?" asked Gracie

"Oh nothing, I'm just happy for the both of you" answered Joe.

Gracie and Buck walked over to where the wedding rings were displayed under the glass counter top. After a few minutes of "oohing" and "ahhing" from Gracie, and "it's nice" or "it's okay" from Buck, Joe walked up and placed a small black velvet box on the counter top.

"Whats this?" asked Gracie

With that same look on his face as before, Joe said "A number of years back a young woman walked in here and was trying on rings. Said she was going to marry this certain man someday. Said this was the ring she wanted. She would come in and try it on…

Gracie's hands went to her face and her fingers covered her lips as she started to cry.

…the years went by and she would come in less and less, until she finally stopped coming at all."

Joe looked at Buck and said "This is the ring you want to buy your bride, she picked it out a long time ago" and handed it to Buck.

Buck took the ring in his hands and slowly opened the small velvet lid and light exploded into the room. Turning the box towards Gracie, who by this time was almost bawling, he asked her again "Will you marry me?" Gracie was physically shaking when Buck took the most beautiful diamond ring he had ever seen from the box and placed it on her left ring finger. As they hugged each other Joe quietly wiped the tears from his cheeks.

After gaining some composure Gracie said "I can't believe you saved this all this time" as she raised her hand and looked at the ring again.

"I knew how much that ring meant to you, and I couldn't have sold it to anyone else, it was already claimed" said Joe with a smile.

"Well you have sure made our day just that much more special, thank you" said Gracie as she gave Joe a big hug.

"Well, shoot, that was worth holding that for you" said Joe with a laugh.

"Yeah, thank you, that was really special of you" said Buck

"Now the wedding rings, anything special catch your eye?" asked Joe

Buck and Gracie looked at each other and then at Joe "What do you suggest?" asked Gracie.

"Well, most people just get solid gold bands, probably the best idea" said Joe.

"What do you think, darling?" Gracie asked Buck

"Sounds good to me" answered Buck

"Solid gold bands it is" said Gracie to Joe.

After Gracie was sized for her ring, she walked over to a mirror and paraded her hand in front of herself. Joe sized Buck's finger as Buck asked "How much is that ring?"

Same price it was when she first tried it on, $699.00" answered Joe

"You are an amazing man, Mr. Stewart!" exclaimed Buck.

Gracie walked back over and put her arm around Buck's waist as Buck handed Joe a check for the total amount "Thank you again, Mr. Stewart."

"No, thank you, and I wish you both years of happiness and prosperity" said Joe.

All the way back to Gracie's, her hand never stopped rising from her lap to extended out in front of her face and back again.

Chapter Thirty-One

Cowboy was wiping the last of the gravy off his plate with a crust of bread when the waitress walked up and asked "Will there be anything else I can get you guys?"

Cowboy looked across at BJ and asked "You want any desert or anything?"

BJ leaned back in his chair and rubbed his belly and answered "Nothing for me, I'm about to pop!"

Cowboy looked at the waitress and said "Just the bill, please"

"Boy, that sure was good, I don't have a lot of money, but I would like to help pay for my meal" said BJ.

"Now, you don't worry about that. It's payment enough having your company along" said Cowboy.

The check came and the pair walked up to the cash register. As Cowboy opened his wallet, BJ noticed a picture of children.

After using the restroom BJ walked out and climbed into the rig where Cowboy was waiting.

"Well, you ready to get on the road again?" asked Cowboy

"Ready and willing" answered BJ.

"There aren't any stops between here and Wichita, it's all turnpike right up to the city limits, just want to make sure" said Cowboy

A few miles had passed when Cowboy looked over at BJ and noticed him yawn. "Kind of funny how a full belly will make you sleepy" said Cowboy

BJ straightened up from his slouched position and said "I'm not sleepy, I was just noticing how flat it is out here."

"Oh its flat, alright, stays this way till just north of Wichita, then you have a few hills, then it flattens out again and stays that way. All the east half of Nebraska is flat, but the western half is what they call the Sand Hill region. You go northwest and you get into the Black Hills, that is where Mt. Rushmore is. Ever been to Mt. Rushmore?" Looking over at BJ for an answer, Cowboy had to smile. BJ had succumbed to the full stomach road fever. He was sleeping like a baby.

Gracie had just unlocked the front door and had no more than taken a couple of steps inside when the phone rang. Reaching the phone on the second ring and raising the receiver to her ear, she said "Hello."

"Hello, this is Ben Williams calling from Houston, Texas" said Ben.

"Oh! Hello again, I'm sorry, can you wait a moment while I get Bobby, he's just outside?" asked Gracie

"Sure, no problem" answered Ben

Gracie set the phone down on the table and raced towards the back door, as she was about half-way across the kitchen floor the back door opened and Buck walked in.

"Buck...hurry, the man from Houston is on the phone!" exclaimed Gracie

"Okay...okay don't have a hemorrhage, Honey" said Buck

Raising the phone to his ear Buck said "Hello, this is Bob."

"Yes, this is Ben Williams in Houston, I received a call from CPS earlier and was given this number to call" said Ben.

"Yes, sir, my name is Bob Stephens, Bill Stephens' brother.

"Mr. Stephens, I am so glad to hear from you. I am so sorry about your brother, he was a good man." said Ben.

"Thank you, sir, I wish I could have been there. Bill and I had not been on the greatest of terms for quite a number of years. Of which now I truly regret, but what I am calling about is my nephew Bill Junior. Is he there?" asked Buck

"Oh my God...no he isn't...I was hoping he was with you, we haven't seen him in three days now!" exclaimed Ben

"Three days!" said Buck angrily.

"What is it?" asked Gracie who was sitting next to Buck.

"He has been gone for three days Baby" said Buck looking over at Gracie.

"We went to bed Wednesday night and the boys were playing a game in my son's room. When we got up, I went to work assuming the boys were sleeping. My wife went up and woke up my son around noon and told him to wake up BJ. After about twenty minutes my wife went back up and woke my son up again. Going by BJ's room, she knocked, and when there was no response, she opened the door and BJ was not there." Ben explained.

"And what happened then?" asked Buck

Ben continued "My wife went back into my son's room and asked Chipper, that's my son's name, if he knew where BJ was and all he said was he didn't know. Not thinking anything of it, figuring he was out playing somewhere, my wife didn't call me. When I got home that night both the boys were not home. My son had told my wife he was going to go find BJ and mess around. Later that evening Chipper came home and we asked where BJ was. He said he hadn't been able to find him"

"And what did you do then" said Buck with exasperation in his voice.

"Well, we waited until it got dark, and when BJ still hadn't shown up, we called the police. They came and asked all of us a lot of questions. The police checked all the local hangouts, the river and parks, they even went to the cemetery where your Brother is buried. Of course they didn't find him. Child Protective Services came by on Friday and raised quite a stir when he couldn't be found. After questioning us for quite a while and threatening to put us in jail for interfering with their duties, "Chipper told them he had run away." explained Ben

"Ran away where, I know he is not with you!" said Buck

"I think it might be better if you talk to my son, he has told everybody that BJ said he was going to go to the ship channel here in Houston and get a job on a ship, and Chipper has stuck to that story with everyone including his mother and me. None of us really believe this. Maybe you talking to him will bring out the truth" said Ben

"Is he there, put him on the phone" said Buck, with just a hint of anger in his voice.

"I don't want you hollering at my son, Mr. Stephens, I won't have that!" said Ben sternly.

"No, No I won't holler at him, could I please talk to him?" asked Buck

"Just a second, he is up in his room, I'll have to get him" said Ben.

Buck took the receiver from his ear and said "This guy says his son, who I guess is BJ's best friend, has been telling everyone that BJ hopped a slow boat to China or something like that, and that no one believes this kid" explained Buck to Gracie as he returned the phone to his ear.

"A slow boat to China, what the…

"Hello" said a small voice on the other end of phone.

"Hello, little fella, this is BJ's Uncle Bill, I understand your BJ's best friend" said Buck

"Yes sir, friends forever" answered Chipper

"I was talking to your father and I am trying to find BJ Are you sure BJ was going to go on a ship?" asked Buck

Looking up at his Dad and then at his Mother, who had now entered the room, Chipper decided he had better tell the truth, even if it meant grounded "The rest of his natural life" as his Dad had threatened so many times before.

"No. He is hitchhiking up to you, Mr. Stephens" Chipper said.

"WHAT!!" was heard in the background as both of Chipper's parents said it in unison. "What are you saying, Chipper" asked Buck with noted anxiety in his voice.

"He left out late Wednesday night, said he didn't want to get put in one of those State schools and was going to go up to Nebraska to see if he could find you. He said you were the only family he had now. He asked me to tell the story about the ship job to give him a head start on the cops. He is my best friend. I tried to talk him out of it, to just wait till you came for him. He said he didn't even know you and that you might not ever come. So he is coming to you. We figured twelve days walking, but BJ said he wasn't walking and should be there in two days. But I guess he hasn't made it yet" said Chipper.

"No...he hasn't made it, do you know how dangerous it is hitchhiking?" asked Buck

"No, sir, I don't even know how" said Chipper in a choked voice.

Taking the phone from his son's ear and raising it to his own Ben said "I am so sorry, Mr. Stephens, we had no idea. Is there anything we can do?"

"I appreciate everything you have already done for BJ I guess you should inform the authorities, and maybe they can find him if he is still in Texas. I am sorry to say this, but I don't even know what he looks like to describe him to the authorities up here" said Buck

"Well, he just turned fourteen, has shocking red hair which he always covers with a ball cap when he is outside. Stands about four and a half feet high and I would guess around a hundred and ten pounds soaking wet. Not a big kid, I guess about average. I don't know if this will help, but he really favors Emily, his Mother." answered Ben

"You knew Emily?" asked Buck

"Your brother, Emily and BJ have been our neighbors for years. BJ and Chipper have been friends all their lives. They were truly beautiful people" answered Ben

"This may sound like a stupid question...but I need to know...were they happy living there in Houston?" asked Buck

"Oh, I can say without a doubt, up until the time Emily was killed, you couldn't find a more completely happy family. After Emily died, I think something died inside of Bill. He was just starting to come around to being the old Bill when this tragedy happened. Just a real shame it is." answered Ben

"Well, I want to thank you for your help, please call me if you hear anything, and if you give me your number, I will call you" said Buck.

Ben gave Buck his number and said "BJ is a fine young man and we will miss him, he is like family to us. If you wouldn't mind, would you have him call us when he shows up?" asked Ben.

"Sure thing, Ben, Goodbye" said Buck

"Goodbye" said Ben and hung up the receiver. Looking at his son he said in a stern voice "You, young man, are grounded for the rest of your natural life."

As Buck hung up the phone he stood and walked into the kitchen. Standing by the kitchen sink and looking out the window he felt a soft touch on his back. Without looking over at Gracie he began "That little fella is out there somewhere hitchhiking."

"Oh my God" exclaimed Gracie.

"Wouldn't even do any good to go looking for him, we don't know which way he is coming, and we could pass him going south as he is riding north in some vehicle" said Buck just above a whisper.

Gracie could hear Buck's voice cracking and softly rubbed circles on his back.

"I have done my fair share of hitching and not all drivers out there are decent people, there are predators out there just looking for young kids to prey on." Buck continued.

"He is going to be alright, Honey" said Gracie trying to sooth Buck. Then she said a quiet prayer as they stood staring out across the hills.

Chapter Thirty-Two

Cowboy rolled north on the Turnpike, crossed the Arkansas River in Wichita and traveled across those hills he had told BJ about. He was just coming up on the exit to McPherson, Kansas when he saw BJ sit up from his sleeping position.

"Well, good morning, young man" said Cowboy

"Morning?" asked BJ.

"Just joking" said Cowboy

BJ reached up and wiped the string of drool from his chin as he stretched his arms out to either side and asked "Where we at?"

We are around fifty miles north of Wichita and about thirty miles south of Salina" answered Cowboy.

"Already, how long have I been sleeping?" asked BJ.

"A little over three hours, probably would have been in Salina by now, but got caught up in a little traffic in Wichita." answered Cowboy

Looking out the side window BJ exclaimed "WOW, what is all that!"

"Sunflowers, BJ, they grow them here like they grow corn in other states" answered Cowboy.

What BJ was looking at was miles and miles of full grown sunflowers all facing the sun which was on the left side of the road. Millions of yellow and white flowers. On the opposite side of the road it was solid Green since you were looking at the backside of the sunflowers.

"That is truly too cool for words" said BJ with a big smile on his face.

"Yeah, it truly is remarkable" said Cowboy

"What do they do with them?" asked BJ.

"You haven't ever eaten any sunflower seeds?" asked Cowboy

"Oh man, I love them."

"They are also used to make cooking oil" stated Cowboy

"Man, I wish my buddy, Chipper, was here, he would want to stop and pick him a bunch. He loves sunflower seeds!" said BJ.

"You have to cook them first" said Cowboy

"Chipper wouldn't care" BJ said, and they both laughed at this.

"Yeah, my kids all like those seeds, too" exclaimed Cowboy

"I noticed back at the truck stop that you had a picture of kids in your wallet when you opened it, how many you got?" asked BJ.

"Well, I have four. There's Justin he's the oldest, then Christian and Ryan, that's my boys.

Then there's Ashtyn Brianna, she's the youngest." answered Cowboy proudly.

"That's a lot of kids, I was an only child" stated BJ.

"Was?" asked Cowboy

"Yeah, my parents are dead" said BJ.

"Sorry to hear that, little fella. Chris told me a little bit about you back at the diner. I really hope things turn out alright for you. I'll remember you in my prayers", said Cowboy.

"You say prayers?" asked BJ.

"Well don't be so shocked, I say them every morning asking for guidance and direction in my day. I asked for a safe and peaceful day for my wife, my children, my mom and dad, my brothers and sisters and their children, my grandparents when they were alive, and, finally, for my aunts and uncles and their children. If I come across anybody during my day that looks like they are not doing to well, I shoot a prayer at them, usually just "God bless them and make their day better." Answered Cowboy.

"Did you shoot any at me?" BJ asked

Cowboy smiled and said "A couple"

A few more miles passed and BJ began to wiggle around in his seat "How long before the next rest stop?" asked BJ.

"About fifteen miles to the truckstop in Salina. Can you hold on till then?" asked Cowboy.

"Yeah, I just hope it's a quick fifteen miles" answered BJ.

Rolling down the road and knowing how hard it can be waiting for that next rest stop, Cowboy figured he would try to get BJ's mind occupied with something else. "Well, you got your route figured out after you leave Salina, little buddy?" asked Cowboy.

BJ smiled and said "That's what Bear always called me."

"Well now your mine, too, maybe you will remember me and Bear in your prayers" said Cowboy.

"I got a lot of people to remember in my prayers now" said BJ as he reflected over the last three days.

"Reach down in that box there by your feet and pull out that road atlas and see if you can figure out the quickest way to where you're going" said Cowboy

BJ was engrossed in the maps he was looking at when he felt the rig slowing down and noticed Cowboy put on the right turn signal.

Looking out the front window BJ saw the truck stop coming into view. "Looks like we are coming to the end of our journey, BJ. I will get you close as I can to the restrooms" said Cowboy

Cowboy stopped near the terminal and told BJ directions to the restrooms as he climbed out of the truck. After BJ walked around the front of the rig, Cowboy pulled up to one of the diesel pumps and began to be fueled up by the attendant.

BJ walked out to where Cowboy was standing by his truck and Cowboy, turning and seeing BJ just about to him, said "Find everything alright?"

"Yeah, just fine. Guess this is where we say goodbye, right?" asked BJ.

"Well, I don't much like to say 'goodbye', I would rather say 'see you later'. Never know when an old trucker might have a delivery up there around where you're headed.

Why don't you write the name of that town down on a piece of paper. Never know!" said Cowboy

"That's the same thing Bear said" said BJ.

Cowboy got a piece of paper from the attendant and handed it to BJ. As BJ was handing it back to Cowboy, the attendant walked up and handed Cowboy a clipboard with a fuel ticket on it to sign. Cowboy tore off his copy of the ticket and stuck both the copy and BJ's piece of paper in a zippered pouch.

"Well, let's get your stuff out of the rig so we can continue on to our destinations" said Cowboy, trying to muster up some determination.

Standing outside the open passenger side door Cowboy noticed BJ had his sign in his hand.

"Well, in about seventy miles you won't need that sign anymore" said Cowboy.

"That's all it is to Nebraska?" asked BJ

"Yeah, your almost there, did you figure out your route okay?" asked Cowboy, just making small talk.

"Yeah, I go north to Bellville to 36, then west to Lebanon to 281, then I cross into Nebraska and stay on 281 all the way to Erickson which is just east of Burwell." answered BJ.

"Sounds like a good plan" said Cowboy as he stuck out his hand for BJ to shake.

BJ grasped Cowboy's hand and shook it. Letting go, he said "Keep the shiny side up and the greasy side down."

Cowboy grinned and said "Where did you hear that?"

"When I was riding with Bear one of his friends told him that. Bear said it's what you say to someone you like" answered BJ.

"Well you keep your sunny side up, little buddy, gotta go" said Cowboy as he walked BJ around the other side of the rig.

"Won't be many big rigs running up north from here, most all of them head east or west on 70, and the highway plays out to a two lane road just the other side of 70. You be careful who you hook up with. Best if it's a family." said Cowboy as he climbed up in the rig.

Shutting the door and rolling down the window Cowboy said "Good luck in all that you do, its been a pleasure knowing you", and with that Cowboy put the rig in gear and BJ watched as

Cowboy and his rig pulled out of the truck stop and turned to head east on 70.

Chapter Thirty-Three

Looking at where the sun was setting in the sky B.J figured he had between two and a half and three hours of daylight left. Walking back inside the truck stop store BJ purchased three cans of soda and a bag of chips. Stopping by the water fountain, he filled up with water, since he had no idea how far it would be to the next place to get a drink. He hoped the sodas would help him between stops. He only had to look back to his walk in Texas to remember not to get caught with nothing to drink.

BJ walked out to the highway, and looking north, he could see the I-70 overpass and he thought to himself "Well if what Cowboy said is true there won't be any truckers on the other side of that bridge." BJ adjusted the straps on his backpack, pulled his cap down a little further on his head, and started walking.

Crossing under the overpass the land ahead seemed to take on a gentle rolling pattern, nothing steep, but definitely not as flat as what lay behind him. Cowboy definitely knew his roads. Shortly, after about two miles the other side of the overpass, the road became a two lane road and traffic was definitely lighter. Every now and then a car, or most often a pickup, would go by, and B.J would just stick out his thumb. At first he would stop at the sound of an approaching vehicle and turn and face the vehicle and put out his thumb, but as the day was winding its way towards dusk, he would continue walking forward and just stick out his thumb.

More than a ride, a place to stop for the night was becoming a priority. BJ was scouring the fields and horizons hoping to find a barn or house where he could ask to stay in the garage. The night birds were starting their calls and more and more bugs seemed to be swarming around BJ when, just before the last light of day, BJ spotted a small bridge ahead. The bridge was no longer than twenty feet and only crossed a minimal creek, probably more a drainage ditch than a creek, but it would be shelter from the rain and morning dew.

BJ walked off the road and down the small embankment to the edge of the trickling water. Stooping over, BJ tried to see under the bridge but the light was fading fast. BJ started stomping loudly as he approached the side of the bridge, thinking this would scare off any snakes or other animals that might be under the bridge. Finding himself a good ten feet under the cover of the bridge and minimal weeds under here, he quickly laid out his blanket while he could still see. In a matter of five minutes BJ could hardly see his hand in front of his face.

Sitting cross legged on his blanket, BJ sat and listened to the night as he consumed some of the chips and drank one of his sodas. Taking the other two cans out of the pack and feeling for a level place to set them, and folding the chips closed and setting the bag by the sodas, BJ settled in for the night.

Rolled up in his blanket BJ had to sleep with his head covered due to the hungry mosquitoes that had also settled in for the night. After what seemed like an eternity, BJ was finally able to fall off to sleep. BJ was totally unaware of the visitors that had inspected him that night. The two opossums passed the lump on the ground without the slightest sense of curiosity. A skunk family passed by with one of the younger skunks walking up and sniffing the bottom of the lump. Luckily BJ hadn't decided to move his feet and scare the young skunk. The raccoon, on the other hand, being a more curious animal than the others decided to investigate the lump. Walking around the lump, sniffing here and sniffing there, it came across the bag of chips. To the raccoon he had struck pay-dirt.

The sound of singing birds and a call to nature brought BJ out of a restless sleep. Pulling the blanket from his head, BJ looked like he had been slapped on both cheeks from the red splotches on them from scratching the numerous assaults from mosquitoes. His hair was all askew and his eyes were slightly swollen from a very restless night.

Running his hands across his face and through his hair, BJ opened his eyes again trying to regain their focus. BJ let a small gasp cross his lips. Lying on his back and looking up at the underside of the bridge BJ, noticed the entire structure was covered in spider webs.

BJ slowly raised only his head and searched the immediate area for any spiders on the ground, as he could see what seemed like hundreds scurrying around the beams of the bridge. Where BJ's head was, there was only about two and a half feet of clearance between the ground and the bottom of the bridge. Looking down at his feet, and since he was lying on a gentle slope towards the water, there was considerably more distance between his feet and the bottom of the bridge.

Still on his back BJ turned his head to the right and using his elbows started lifting his torso only inches and squirmed himself slowly around to where he was parallel with the water. This took what seemed like forever. Every time he would move a couple of inches and would turn to lookup at the bridge, he would see spiders with large bloated brown or black bodies scurry into holes built into the wooden beams. BJ would close his eyes and squirm a couple of more inches. Finally with his head and feet parallel with the water, BJ rolled down towards the water. After a couple of rolls, and with now about six feet between the ground and the bottom of the bridge, BJ sat up and let out a deep breath.

After a moment BJ reached down and untangled the blanket that had balled up around his feet. BJ stood up to a crouched position and took a couple of steps down towards the water before standing erect. A little shiver crossed his back and BJ started rapidly rubbing his hands along opposite arms, his chest, and back and down both pants legs. After assuring himself there were no spiders on him, BJ calmed down.

"Man, that was truly freaky" said BJ to himself.

Looking back up the slope BJ saw his backpack, ball cap, and one can of soda. Seeing the soda brought on a tremendous thirst in BJ. Moving back up the slope, first at a crouch and then to crawl, BJ stretched out and grabbed his cap, pack, and finally the can of soda and moved backwards back down the slope. Back at the bottom BJ dropped the pack at his feet, slapped his ball cap a couple of times on his leg and, after inspecting it, placed it on his head. At the same time, he heard a thrashing in the brush and looked up to see two deer running away from the creek into the trees.

"Wow, how cool!" said BJ out loud.

Standing there for a few more seconds looking to see if he would see the deer again, BJ was reminded how thirsty he was. Pulling his shirt tail from his pants BJ wiped the dirt from the top of the can, popped the top and greedily drank half the contents before removing the can from his lips. With his thirst satisfied

BJ held his soda in his left hand and reached down and slipped his right hand through the straps of his backpack, grabbed a corner of his blanket, and dragged it behind him as he walked out into the sunshine. Standing in the sunlight BJ looked down at himself and was amazed at how dirty he was. "Man, I need to clean up, nobody is going to pick me up looking like this!" said BJ to himself.

BJ carefully picked up the blanket by two corners and shook it out and then rolled it up. Setting it by his pack BJ carefully opened his backpack and pulled out his other set of clothes. After shaking them out in case a spider had decided to make a home in them, he set them on top of his blanket.

BJ walked down to the creek and looked downstream towards where the deer had been and noticed what looked like an area where the trees seemed wider apart. "Well, maybe the creek is a little wider there" thought BJ.

Walking downstream through some heavy brush and around trees, BJ came into a little clearing. The creek had definitely widened here to form a small pond. Out of sight of the road BJ stripped down and stepped into the water. Goosebumps immediately sprung up all over his body as the water was very cool.

"This ain't going to happen!" exclaimed BJ as he jumped out of the water back on the shore.

Remembering his Biology class BJ thought to himself "This has to be spring fed to be so cold."

Looking at his arms and hands and how dirty they were, he could only imagine how dirty his face must be after sleeping in the dirt under that bridge. BJ leaned over the edge of the water and in the calm reflection looking back at him he saw the disheveled hair and what he thought was dirt, the red splotches on his face.

"Ain't nobody going to pick me up looking like this, might as well get this over" said BJ.

Stepping back into the water with his arms wrapped across his chest, BJ slowly walked into deeper water. By the time the water reached mid-thigh BJ was shaking uncontrollably.

"There is only one way to do this, buddy" thought BJ as he remembered going to the pool with Chipper, and the best way was to just jump in all at once. With that thought in mind BJ squatted down in the water.

"OH MY GOD!" shouted BJ as he sprung back up to a standing position.

Experience had taught him though that he had to stay in the water to get used to it. After a couple of more dunks BJ did become used to the temperature and washed himself the best he could without soap.

Dressed again and with his backpack back on his shoulders, BJ remembered he had another soda under the bridge. Taking his pack back off BJ walked down by the water and went back under the bridge. Being later in the day and much lighter under the bridge it wasn't quite as eerie to BJ.

Walking along the water BJ spotted his other can laying near the water where it had rolled to during the night. Picking it up and dunking it into the water to wash it off, BJ spotted his chip bag torn into small pieces.

'Wow!!...I had forgotten about them, wonder what got those?" said BJ as he looked around and a small shiver ran along his spine.

"I think its time to get out of here" said BJ loudly hoping to scare anything away that might be watching him.

Chapter Thirty-Four

BJ stood up on the other side of the bridge for a few minutes waiting for the first vehicle to come along.

"Looks like its going to be a slow day" said BJ to himself.

Looking back to the south and seeing nothing moving, BJ started walking. After about thirty minutes, and a good mile from the bridge, BJ heard a vehicle approaching from the south. BJ stopped and turned towards the approaching vehicle and stuck out his thumb. The only response BJ received was a blast from the horn and a cloud of dust as BJ had to step further off the road to avoid being hit.

"Thanks a lot, Jerk!" said BJ angrily as he waved his arms in front of his face clearing the cloud.

A few minutes went by and BJ heard another vehicle approaching. Turning to look BJ saw an old pickup truck with a horse trailer behind it. Stepping off the road a little more than the last time, BJ stuck out his thumb.

The truck slowed down and came to a stop with the horse trailer directly in front of BJ. Looking up into the truck BJ noticed three men all wearing cowboy hats. The man on the passenger side leaned out and hollered "Come on, if you want a ride!"

Running up to the passenger side door BJ looked in and asked "How far you guys going?"

"Well, son, if we weren't going but five miles up the road, it would be better than standing here, wouldn't it?" said the driver.

"Well, yes Sir, it would" said BJ.

"We are going up just past Belleville, how about you?" asked the man in the middle.

"Belleville is where I'm heading, sure would appreciate a ride there" said BJ exuberantly. "Get yourself in the back" said the driver.

"Thanks, mister" said BJ as he climbed in the back and rolled over onto his side as the truck took off rapidly before he was settled.

A little over an hour had passed when BJ noticed the truck slowing down and stopping right on the highway. "This is where you get off, boy" shouted the driver.

BJ grabbed his stuff and jumped off the passenger side of the truck. Standing on the side of the road BJ barely had time to holler "thanks" when the truck pulled away. The man on the passenger side stuck his arm out the window and waved.

BJ waved back and watched as the truck and trailer crested the hill and was gone. Standing there at the intersection of two highways and nothing else, BJ spotted a sign across the road he had been on. Walking across the street he read the sign that was put up for people headed south. BJ figured the one for him must have been knocked down or something.

The sign read "Belleville 5" with an arrow pointing east on top, and below that was "Lebanon 42" with an arrow pointed west. Looking to his right BJ saw a tall hill in front of him and a highway sign with 36 and a smaller sign below it on the same pole that said west.

BJ turned west and started walking and thought to himself "Well, that's one more highway behind me, no more 81 for me."

BJ had only walked between five and ten minutes, and was just coming to the top of the hill, when a car came through the intersection he had just left. BJ heard the car almost too late as he had been walking a little too far out into the street. The young girl driving the car fortunately had seen BJ and honked as she got closer. BJ nearly jumped out of his skin at the sound of the horn and leapt to the side of the road and fell down. The young girl slammed on her brakes and stopped right beside BJ, who was now picking himself up from the ground.

"Are you alright?" asked the young girl through the open passenger window. B.J was swatting the dirt off his pants with his cap when he angrily said "You ought to…and then he looked at her and smiled…I'm alright, just a little scraped."

"Well, I thought you would have heard me coming, I didn't mean to scare you like that" said the girl.

"I guess I had my mind on other things" said BJ.

"Well look, can I give you a ride?" said the girl.

"Why sure, I would appreciate that" said BJ as he opened the car door.

"Just throw your things in the back seat" said the girl.

BJ took off his backpack and opened the rear door and set his things on the back seat. Climbing into the front seat BJ offered his hand and said "Bob Stephens, Jr." The girl took his hand and shook it and said "Lucinda Ann, but everybody calls me Cindy."

"Yeah my friends call me BJ" said BJ.

"Well then, BJ it is. Where you headed?" asked Cindy

"Up into Nebraska to see my uncle" answered BJ.

"That could be close or that could be far, what part of Nebraska?" asked Cindy

"You ever heard of Burwell?" asked BJ.

"Burwell…yeah, I think that's the town my older brother went to work in a couple of summers ago" answered Cindy.

"Really!" said BJ with noted excitement in his voice.

Cindy put the car in drive and proceeded driving down the road. Looking over at BJ with a scowl on her face she said "I have never heard anybody get excited about Burwell."

"Its just that your the first person I have talked to that has even heard of Burwell" explained BJ.

"So, you're not from around here, I take it" said Cindy

BJ looked out the passenger window and thought for a second or two before deciding that Cindy was just a kid, too, and it wouldn't do any harm to let her in on a little of his story. Looking back over at the young girl driving, he told her about his uncle and dad. After he finished telling her of his last three days on the road, they both sat silently as the car sped along the highway.

"So both of your parents are gone, and you don't even know if your uncle still lives in Burwell?" asked Cindy with a sadness in her voice."

"Yeah, that's about it, and if he does live there, I don't even know if he will want me to stay with him. My dad and my uncle had a falling out long before I was born and never had a chance to make things right before my dad was killed. I have never even met him, much less talked to him" explained BJ.

"That's awful, my dad always tells me there is no time like the present, but that usually applies to chores. I can see where that saying applies to much more." said Cindy

"Anyway, I am glad I can be of help. How far were you planning on going down 36?" asked Cindy.

"Let me see," said BJ as he pulled the paper from his pocket that he had written his route down on.

"Says I take 36 to Lebanon and pick up 281 north all the way through Grand Island, Nebraska." answered BJ.

"Well, I guess that's one way up there, but I am going to Phillipsburg, that's where I live. I used to hear my dad and Mike, that's my older brother, talk about how it was a straight shot from Phillipsburg to Burwell. Might help you some." stated Cindy.

"So how far is your home town?" asked BJ.

"About another forty-five minutes to an hour" answered Cindy.

"I guess you wouldn't know how far Burwell is from there?" asked BJ.

"From what Mike used to say, a couple of hours. That could be any where from one hundred and twenty to one hundred and fifty miles, depending on how fast he drove." answered Cindy

The pair drove along in silence for a while, seeing a sign for Lebanon and a sign just below it say "Geographical center of the 48 Continental United States" made BJ look over at Cindy. BJ didn't even have to ask.

"There is a stone monument just north of Lebanon that marks the exact center of the forty eight states" stated Cindy.

"Cool," responded BJ, without much enthusiasm.

The conversation between the two went from music to movies to talking about Houston. Cindy was just in awe of all that BJ had done. When Cindy asked BJ what a mall was, BJ knew he was in for a new way of life for sure.

Pulling into Phillipsburg, which was a relatively small town, Cindy asked BJ if he would like to come home and have some lunch, which BJ politely refused stating he would like to try to make it to Burwell today and would need all the daylight he had left.

Cindy pulled through Phillipsburg and took BJ to a gas station on the outskirts of town and pulled in.

"Well, I guess this is as far as we go, BJ," said Cindy as she parked the car in front of the station.

BJ looked around and saw a sign that had 183 and a white arrow pointing north. "I want to thank you, and I wish I had something I could give you" said BJ, looking over at Cindy.

"I really enjoyed your company on the ride home, that's payment enough" said Cindy with a smile.

BJ opened the door and climbed out, then opened the back door and retrieved his pack. Closing both doors BJ leaned inside the front window and extended his right hand and shook Cindy's and said something Cindy would never forget. "Enjoy your life, it is the only one you have."

BJ waved as Cindy backed out of the parking place and turned back towards Phillipsburg. And when she turned to wave back to him, he thought he saw a small tear rolling down her cheek as she smiled and pulled away.

BJ stood there with his pack at his feet and holding his sign in his left hand, he watched as Cindy went over the top of the hill and was out of sight. With a deep sigh BJ thought "I am sure getting tired of people leaving me."

BJ turned and picked up his pack and walked to the door of the station. Setting his pack down BJ propped his sign up against the pack and proceeded through the front door. Inside the station BJ was amazed at how much this station reminded him of Cotton's back in Texas. As BJ walked across the wooden floor, every now and then one of the boards would squeak under his weight. Standing in front of the soda machine and reading the labels from top to bottom, BJ's eyes lit up when he saw Nehi Grape. Reaching into his pocket BJ pulled out two quarters and put them in the slot. Opening the glass vertical door on the machine, BJ spotted the bottle in its own little holder directly across from the label on the machine.

BJ pulled the bottle from the holder and tried to twist the cap from the bottle. A man standing behind the cash register, seeing BJ struggling, said "You have to use the opener."

BJ, slightly startled, turned at the sound of the man's voice, and seeing the man pointing, turned and saw one of those same little boxes inside the machine that Cotton had on the outside of his. BJ put the bottle in the box and popped the cap off the bottle. Putting the bottle to his lips BJ was again amazed at how the aroma of the grape was so strong. Pulling the bottle away from his lips after a few good swallows, BJ turned towards the man and said "Thanks."

Walking over towards the man, BJ stopped at the candy counter and picked out a couple of candy bars and then proceeded on to the counter.

"How much do I owe you?" asked BJ as he laid the bars on the counter.

"Lets see…that will be eighty-three cents with tax" answered the man behind the counter.

BJ reached back into his pocket and pulled out the few dollar bills he had crumpled together. He pulled one away from the rest and handed it to the man.

As the man was making change, BJ asked "You wouldn't know how far it is to Taylor up 183, would you?"

"About one hundred and thirty miles, young man, that where you headed?" asked the man. "Actually, I'm going to Burwell" said BJ.

"Burwell, been there a few times myself, used to work up at the feed lot in the summer when I was in high school" said the man behind the counter.

"Really!…how far is Burwell from Taylor?" asked BJ.

"Fifteen miles, where you coming from?" asked the man.

Not wanting to let too much information out, BJ came up with the first place he could think of, "Around Belleville," BJ said, and he could see the man's eyes change to a dullness and he kind of dropped his chin a little.

"I'm sorry, did I say something wrong?" asked BJ.

The man looked back up at BJ and said "Oh no, it's just that hearing the name of that town reminds me of my sister. She was killed in a wreck at the intersection of 36 and 81 a couple of years ago. An eighteen wheeler hit her broadside. She was heading home when it happened."

"I'm sorry" said BJ.

"Oh no, that's alright, I know she is in a better place today, anything else I can do for you?" asked the man behind the counter.

"No, thank you, I better get on my way" said BJ.

The man looked out into the front, and not seeing any cars asked" Are you hitchhiking?" "Yes sir" answered BJ.

"Well you be careful, and the name's Mike" said the man behind the counter.

Chapter Thirty-Five

BJ walked around the side of the station and used the restroom, washed his hands and face figuring he would get a ride easier if he was clean. Coming out of the restroom BJ strapped his backpack on his shoulders, walked out to 183 and proceeded on the last leg of his journey.

After half an hour had passed, and a little over a mile north of 36, BJ decided to stop and eat one of his candy bars and wait for someone to come by. Not one single vehicle had passed going north, and the only thing going south had been a farmer on a tractor who had waved at him as he went by.

Sitting on his pack and having finished his candy bar, BJ started thinking maybe he had made a mistake taking this highway when he saw a car heading towards him from the south. The car started slowing down even before BJ put out his thumb, and BJ thought that was kind of strange. The car stopped right on the highway and a middle aged man rolled down the electric window and said "Come on and get in, I'll take you wherever you want to go." Then he smiled just a little too big.

BJ remembered what Bear and Cowboy both had said about being careful, and to try to ride with families, and responded "No thank you, I'm waiting on someone."

"Oh come on, you aren't waiting on anybody, get in and we will have some fun" said the man in a soothing voice and then winked at BJ.

BJ picked up his backpack and started walking towards the rear of the car and the man put his car in reverse and backed up to where BJ had stopped. BJ could feel a lump starting to grow in his throat.

"Come on little fella, I know you are lying to me. I'll give you fifty dollars if you will just keep me company," said the man more sternly as he reached for his door handle and started opening his car door to get out.

"Man, why don't you just get out of here" said BJ with a noticeable crack in his voice. "Oh yeah" said the man as he smiled at B. J. and started to step out of his car.

In their conversation neither the man nor BJ were aware of the pickup truck that was pulling up behind the man's car till the truck honked his horn.

At the sound of the horn, the man jumped back behind the steering wheel, slammed the car door, and drove off blowing a kiss to BJ as he pulled away.

The pickup pulled up to where BJ was standing, and a woman on the passenger side looked out the window and asked "Are you all right honey?"

BJ was visibly shaken and in an unsteady voice replied "Yes, Maam, I am sure glad you guys came along. I don't think that guy is a very nice man."

"Well, what are you doing out here?" asked the woman.

"I'm trying to get to my uncle's house" answered BJ.

"Well, honey, how far is that, maybe we can take you, right Mac?" said the woman as she looked at the man behind the wheel.

"Whatever you say, Martha" said the man behind the wheel

"Do you know where Taylor, Nebraska is?" asked BJ.

"Well, no I don't, is it near Kearny, that's where we are headed" asked the woman.

Remembering his map and where Kearny was, BJ replied "Yes, Maam, Taylor is just north of Interstate 80 on 183" answered BJ.

"Well, you will have to ride in the back, there is no room up here" said the woman. Looking down the road towards the direction the man took off in, BJ said "I don't have a problem with that at all, thank you very much."

BJ threw his pack and sign up in the bed of the truck, climbed in and sat down with his back up against the cab of the truck.

"You alright back there, honey?" asked the woman as she wiped her cheek where something had just brushed it.

"Yes, Maam, I'm fine" answered BJ.

The trio hadn't gone more than four miles when BJ saw the car with the man in it pass them heading back to where they had come from, and a shiver ran down BJ's spine. BJ knew that the man was most likely going back to see if he was still there and possibly hurt him. BJ lowered his head and silently said "Thank you, God."

BJ sat in the back watching the scenery go by, mostly corn fields and every now and then a farm house and barn. BJ was very glad that the end of his trip was near. After about a half an hour had passed BJ was looking out to his right and a large white sign appeared and on the sign were the words "Welcome to Kansas", BJ turned to his left and leaned up on the side of the truck bed just in time to see "Welcome to Nebraska" and below that read "The Cornhusker State." BJ watched as that sign got further and further behind them before he resumed his sitting position in the back of the truck. "I finally made it" BJ thought to himself, and a broad smile crossed his face.

Another hour had passed and every time they would pass through a small town that had a stop light or stop sign in it (which wasn't very often), Martha would holler back at him, "You doing alright back there?" and BJ's response was always "just fine, Maam." BJ was noticing how there were more cattle around here than there had been in Kansas, when all of a sudden the truck was pulling off into a parking lot.

BJ put his weight on his left hand and turned to his left still sitting and looked out through the front window and noticed they had pulled into an oversized gas station that could accommodate big rigs as well as cars and he thought, "Alright, maybe I can catch another ride with a trucker heading north."

The pickup pulled to a stop by the front of the station and BJ climbed out of the back of the truck on the driver's side. Walking up to the driver's side window, BJ extended his hand which Mac shook and BJ said "Thank you, Sir, for stopping."

"Glad I could be of help, son, this is where we turn to go on up 80 to Kearney, you want to go on north, so you take care of yourself now."

BJ walked around the front of the truck and up to the passenger side window, and with his pack on his left shoulder and his sign in his left hand, he extended his right hand to Martha which she grabbed and pulled him gently to her and placed a soft kiss on his forehead. Letting him go she said "That's for luck honey, I hope wherever you are headed you find happiness. Just remember it's up to you to be happy where you are, focus on the good things, and don't dwell to long on the bad, and you will be alright" and then she just smiled.

"Thank you, Maam, I'll try to remember that" said BJ.

The pickup truck started to pull away and BJ hollered after them "Thank you and God bless you."

An arm came from both windows and waved. BJ was still waving when the pickup turned right onto the access of I-80.

Walking towards the door of the station BJ heard a voice say "Looks like you made it, son." Turning towards the direction of the voice BJ saw an old man in a beat up old straw cowboy hat and said "Excuse me."

"Your sign there" said the old man pointing at the sign he was carrying.

BJ held the sign up that was definitely the worse for the wear with tears in it and rust and dirt stains on it and said "Yes, Sir, I have" and then he asked "Do you know how far it is to Taylor?"

"About eighty to eighty-five miles" said the old cowboy.

"Thank you, Sir" said BJ.

The old man just reached up and grabbed the brim of his hat and tipped it towards BJ.

BJ walked into the station and purchased a couple of sodas, and noticing his funds were just about depleted had to figure what else he could afford. Still having one can of sardines left, BJ found a box of crackers. After paying for his items BJ only had twenty-seven cents left which he stuffed into his pocket. After Using the restroom and getting a drink from the water fountain, BJ left the station and walked out to the highway and proceeded north one more time.

After crossing the bridge over I-80 BJ noticed a small gas station on the other side of the road from him. BJ stood there for a few minutes and thought "I wonder if Mom and Dad ever stopped there on their way from Burwell to Kearney when they were going to college." BJ felt a little pain in his heart and tear wells formed in his eyes, and as a tear fell from his eye, he said "I miss you guys so much." BJ stood there for a few more minutes watching cars come from the north, cross the bridge and turn east toward Kearney, and he would think "My mom and dad used to do that."

BJ knew this last leg of his trip would be tough, because everything he would see such as bridges, old houses and barns, and the such would have been seen by his parents at one time or the other. At the same time he felt a sudden closeness to his parents. If BJ could have seen into heaven at that very minute he would have seen his parents smiling as they watched him. He would have seen his mother reach and caress his cheek. Instead he felt the tickle of the tear and reached up and wiped it from his cheek. BJ reached down and wiped a dry hand on the front of his pants.

BJ looked towards the north and much like when he crossed I-70, there wasn't anything out there but open country, and BJ once more put one foot in front of the other and headed to what he hoped was home.

BJ looked down at his watch and, noticing the time, knew there might be a chance he would spend one more night sleeping somewhere before he would make it to Burwell. This thought reminded him of the spiders and also of the man in the car. These thoughts made BJ's head heavier and heavier as he walked along and a sadness was beginning to overwhelm him.

BJ had walked another five minutes when he looked up to see where he was going and something moved in the tall grass ahead of him. BJ stopped and tried to see if he could tell what it was. His mind started playing all kinds of games, could be a snake or a skunk. Whatever it was BJ really didn't want to find out. He looked both ways and after a south bound car passed by, he crossed to the other side of the road. Walking cautiously to the point exactly across the road from where he had seen the movement, BJ spotted something yellow flick the air.

"Skunks sure aren't yellow and that wasn't a snake" BJ thought to himself as he stood there for a few more seconds.

BJ made his best attempt at a whistle, and a little head popped up. BJ took a quick look both ways and ran across the street. The little puppy ran the other way and stopped a few feet from where BJ was standing. BJ squatted down and held out his hand and said "Come here boy, come here boy, I won't hurt you."

The puppy cocked his head, first to the right then to his left, and let out a little bark. BJ made kissing noises through pursed lips and the puppy made little bounds towards BJ. BJ reached down and scooped the little puppy up and cradled him in his arms as he stood up, and the puppy started covering BJ's chin and cheeks with licks.

"What are you doing way out here by yourself, little fella?" said BJ as he looked up and down the highway for anyone who might be in the area. Seeing no one, BJ set the puppy back down on the ground. Standing back up straight seemed to be a signal for the puppy to start whining and jumping up on BJ's pants leg. BJ started walking along the highway and the puppy was running as fast as it could to keep up with him, steadily running under his feet until BJ had to stop again.

He looked down at the puppy that was once again jumping up and down and every now and then would manage to get his front paws to rest on BJ's calf. Looking around at the surrounding countryside, BJ noticed not a single house or building anywhere in sight.

"Well, it looks like you and me are in the same boat...alone."

BJ, knowing he wouldn't make very good time with the puppy walking under his feet, slipped the backpack from his shoulders and set it on the ground. The puppy was immediately up on BJ's knee as BJ squatted and opened the flap at the top of the pack. BJ easily scooped up the puppy under its chest, and with its back paws dangling in the air, he gently slid the puppy inside the pack. With the puppy's front legs and head sticking out of the pack, BJ slid the pack over his shoulders, adjusted the position of the straps and started walking up the highway. The puppy watched from his perch for a few steps then turned his head and gave BJ a little lick on the back of

BJ's neck as if to say "Thank you for saving me", then resumed his position, watching the ground go by.

BJ and his new friend had walked another ten minutes up the highway when BJ heard the sound of an approaching vehicle. He turned and looked down the road and was happy to see another pickup truck with a couple of people in it approaching him at high rate of speed, much faster than he would have hoped for.

"These guys may not stop, little buddy" said BJ to his new friend.

BJ stood looking at the approaching vehicle and stuck out his thumb. The truck came nearer and started slowing down, and BJ's heart started beating a little faster. The truck slammed on its brakes and came to a halt a good hundred feet past BJ, an arm came out of the passenger side window and waved him towards the truck. BJ took off at a run as fast as he could with the puppy on his back. Running towards the truck BJ noticed three young guys not much older than him sitting in the truck, all of them looking back as BJ ran to them. When BJ reached the rear of the truck he heard the boy who was now leaning out the passenger side window holler "Go...go...go!" as the driver sped away leaving BJ and the puppy standing in a cloud of dust.

BJ could hear the boys laughing and the horn honking as they drove away. Bent over at the waist and covered in dust that had stuck to the thin film of sweat that had formed on his skin, BJ wanted to curse the boys, but feared if he did they would be back and there were too many of them.

Straightening back up he looked around at the puppy just in time for the puppy to sneeze right in his face. Turning back forward and wiping off the left side of his face, BJ heard the puppy sneeze again. "Well, bless you, little fella, guess they got us both pretty good, huh?"

BJ was wiping the dust off his shirt sleeves and pants when another pickup came slowly up behind him.

BJ jumped a little when the puppy let out a few quick little barks and, turning to look at the puppy, saw the truck coming to a stop beside him.

Two young girls somewhere around six or seven years old and a man in his late twenties were in the front of the truck, the man leaned forward with his arms resting on the steering wheel and asked "What's a young boy like you doing way out here?"

Without hesitation BJ responded "Trying to get to my uncle's in Taylor." It was nice being so close that it didn't sound so outlandish.

"Well, you and your dog got quite a ways to go yet, guess you wouldn't mind a lift" said the man.

"Oh, yes Sir, we would love a ride!" exclaimed BJ.

"Well, climb in the back, we are going to Milton about twenty-five miles up the road, ain't much" said the man

"Hey, that's twenty-five miles closer, thank you very much" said BJ as a big smile crossed his face.

"Climb in the back and we'll get going" said the man.

BJ climbed in over the tailgate, carefully slipped his pack off his back and sat down. The truck pulled away slowly for which BJ was grateful as the puppy had no intentions of staying in the pack once it came off BJ.

BJ sat with his back to the rear window and cradled the puppy in his lap. BJ knew the little girls were looking out the rear window of the truck by the way the puppy kept looking over BJ's shoulder. Every now and then he would hear a tapping on the glass and a giggle would follow.

BJ reached inside his pack and pulled out the single stack of crackers he had bought, and after some trouble opening them with the puppy steadily trying to get his nose in the little box, BJ pulled out a cracker and held it out to the puppy who made quick work out of it.

"Well, little buddy, you must be starving" said BJ as he pulled another one out and repeated the process.

"Yeah, little buddy, that might be a good name for you, I always liked it when Bear and Cowboy called me that" said BJ to his new found friend.

The truck crossed over a small stream and BJ was reminded of last night and decided if he was going to sleep under a bridge it was going to have to be a big one.

What seemed like just a few minutes had passed, the truck pulled to a stop half on and half off the pavement and the man leaned out and said "We are going to turn off right up here, sorry it couldn't have been further."

BJ set the puppy back inside the pack and decided he better not put the crackers in with him as he was trying to eat some more of them as BJ tried to stick them in the pack beside him. BJ stood up and put the pack back over his shoulders, and with crackers in hand, climbed out of the truck. Walking up to the man, BJ reached out his hand and the man shook it. "Thank you again for the ride, Sir."

"You take care of yourself" said the man.

"Is there a store or something up ahead, I want to get my dog something to eat and maybe some water?" asked BJ.

"Well...you aren't too far from the river, about a half a mile, he can get a drink there and Milton is another couple of miles past the river" answered the man.

"Well, thanks again" said BJ and the man waved as the girls hollered "Bye" as the truck pulled up a little ways and turned right up a little country road. BJ stood and watched as a cloud of dust followed the truck up the road.

Adjusting the straps and starting to walk up the road, BJ said "Well we are just that much closer, little buddy."

The road had a slight incline at this point. BJ bent slightly at the waist, put one foot in front of the other, and proceeded up the hill. After a few hundred yards BJ tried to look back over his shoulder at the puppy, not seeing the puppy's head BJ said "You doing all right back there little buddy?".

Hearing BJ's voice the puppy, whose head had been looking down at the ground passing by, lifted his ears and cocked his head up in the direction of the sound. Seeing the puppy's snout out of the corner of his eye, BJ turned his head back forward and with a big smile on his face said "Not much farther."

Coming to the top of the hill BJ stopped and surveyed the surrounding landscape in awe. From the top of the hill lay before him a wide flat valley with a river running through on this side. There were fields on both sides full of nearly mature corn. This ribbon of concrete he was walking on cut straight across the middle to hills rising on the other side. BJ could barely make out a town at the base of the hills. He looked to his right and left and could see little trails of dust here and there caused by different types of vehicles. Looking to his left he noticed the sun was getting low in the sky, and looking back across the valley knew he would never make Milton before dark.

"Well, little buddy, looks like we may have one more night on the road" said BJ.

The road had a little more of a downward slope at this point and BJ was able to stand upright as he walked towards the bridge. Coming up to the bridge BJ said "Well, we could stop here or cross to the other side and be just that much closer in the morning." The puppy, as if responding to BJ, let out a couple of yelps. BJ smiled and said "Okay, we will sleep on the other side."

Standing by the end of the bridge BJ read the sign that said "South Loup River." After walking a short way across the bridge, BJ looked out across the railing and noticing the flat grassy areas on either side of the water, remembered "this is the area the Sioux Indians must have lived" and he let his imagination take hold as he visualized teepees on either side of the river stretching out as far as he could see.

BJ was still casting glances to his right and left nearing the other side of the bridge, when all of a sudden BJ's nostrils were filled with the sweetest aroma. The puppy had also picked up the scent and started whining. The aroma became stronger and stronger as BJ came closer to the end of the bridge. The puppy, maddened by the smell, started trying to climb out of the backpack using BJ's shoulders as if they were rungs on a ladder. The pain inflicted by the puppy's claws caused BJ to remove the pack quickly. Once the pack was on the ground the puppy leapt from the pack and ran around the end of the bridge railing and disappeared beneath the bridge.

"Wait a minute! Come back here!" hollered BJ as he scooped up his pack and ran after the puppy.

Coming around the end of the railing and running cautiously down the slope, BJ noticed the smell was definitely coming from under the bridge. Stopping at the edge of the support beams under the bridge BJ saw a man silhouetted by the setting sun, sitting by a small campfire. BJ also noticed his puppy was right beside the man, and he was eating something on the ground. BJ walked a little further down the slope before he passed under the first beam and said "Gosh, I'm sorry, Mister" and as BJ walked closer the man just looked up and smiled.

"That's quite all right, I gave it to him. I hope you don't mind" said the stranger.

"No, Sir, I don't mind" said BJ as he glanced toward the fire and saw four of the sweetest looking hot dogs skewered on a stick propped over the heat.

Following BJ's gaze the man said "You are welcome to have one if you would like." "Oh!...no sir, I have some food in my pack, I wouldn't want to short you any" said BJ, his eyes never leaving the fire.

"Nonsense, you know as well as I that you can't buy less than six hot dogs to a pack, I have more than enough, I insist!" said the man.

"Well, I guess if you insist" said BJ.

The man reached beside him and produced a bag of hot dog buns and handed them to BJ.

"I'm afraid all I have is ketchup and mustard, I always save these little packets, never know when they will come in handy" said the man as he handed a smaller bag to BJ. BJ took the smaller bag and after dobbing a packet of each on his bun, watched as the man picked up the stick with the hotdogs on it with one hand as the other hand came up with a huge knife. The man pointed the stick towards BJ and, with the blunt side of the knife against the stick behind the hotdogs, pushed them towards the end of the stick. BJ held his bun open and caught the hotdog as it fell from the end of the stick.

In one swooping motion BJ's hand went to his mouth and he bit off a large portion of the hotdog. The puppy having finished his hotdog started smelling around the ground, and not finding anything, immediately sat down beside the man and started whining.

"Be alright if I give him a little more?" asked the man

"Umm-hum" answered BJ, the best he could with his mouth full.

The man produced the big knife again and pulled another hotdog off the stick and stuck it by the puppy's nose. The puppy grabbed it and lay down and started eating it much slower than the first one.

BJ sat down on the other side of the puppy and dug into his pack for a soda. Coming out with the soda, and realizing he only had one, asked "Would you like this?" while holding the can out to the man.

"Have you got two?" asked the man.

"No, Sir, but your welcome to this one" said BJ.

"Tell you what, we can split it" and with that the man lifted a strange looking cup. It was made of tin and was a crescent moon shape. The handle swung up from the side and was also made of tin.

BJ handed the soda to the man and watched as he opened it and poured half of the contents into his strange cup. Taking the soda back from the man BJ asked "What kind of cup is that, looks old?"

"Well it is old, I have had this old cup ever since I was in the Army. It's called a canteen cup. Went along with your canteen" answered the man.

"Would you like another hotdog?" asked the man

BJ looking at the stick and seeing only one hotdog left said "Oh no, Mister! couldn't take your last one."

"Oh don't worry about that, I have already eaten and I have more to cook later" said the man.

"Well, in that case, sure!" said BJ.

By the time BJ finished his second hotdog, the puppy had laid down beside BJ's leg and was sleeping. From the look of the puppy's protruding stomach he was definitely full.

"Well, it looks like somebody is happy" said the man nodding towards the puppy.

"Yes, Sir, and thank you, by the way, my name is BJ" said BJ. introducing himself.

"BJ, that's a good name, what's your dog's name?" asked the man.

"He doesn't really have one yet, just found him today while I was traveling up from Kearney" answered BJ.

"Traveling huh, maybe you could name him after General Lee's horse" said the man.

"You mean General Lee, from the Civil War?" asked BJ.

"You bet, the name of his horse was "Traveler", what do you think?" asked the man. "Traveler…yeah, I like that" said BJ as he reached down beside him and stroked the puppy sleeping beside him.

The pair sat in silence as the light of the day fell to darkness and the light of the campfire took its place. BJ was watching as the man whittled on a piece of wood and stated "I have never seen a knife like that."

"Its called a K-Bar, government issue" said the man.

"You work for the Government?" asked BJ.

"Oh no, got this when I was in the service, in Viet Nam" answered the man.

As if to change the subject the man asked "So, where you headed?"

"Up to my uncle's in Burwell, about another fifty miles north. How about you, you from around here?" asked BJ.

"No…I'm not really from anywhere, been traveling myself for a little over eleven years now. Don't really call anywhere home, that way I'm home anywhere I go" said the man.

"Sounds kind of lonely to me" said BJ.

"Oh, it is never lonely, after we keep each other company tonight, I will find another wayward traveler or lost soul to keep company tomorrow. The good Lord always provides" stated the man.

"Well, I'm getting kind of tired, think I'll lay down" said BJ.

"Yeah, I'm fixing to call it a night myself" said the man

BJ, looking around in what light there was, noticed the man had no blanket.

"Don't you have a blanket or something?" asked BJ.

"No, I am perfectly comfortable in my clothes, thank you" answered the man.

"Okay, but at least use my sign to lay your head on instead of laying in the dirt" pleaded BJ.

"Okay BJ, if it will make you happy" said the man as he took the sign from BJ's offering hand.

Laying down on his side facing where the man had laid down on the other side of the fire, BJ looked at the man and said "Good night and God bless"

"And you too my son" answered the man.

BJ put his arm around "Traveler" and pulled the puppy a little closer to his chest and drifted into the most peaceful sleep he had slept in weeks.

Chapter Thirty-Six

The next morning found Buck sitting at his kitchen table with a cup of coffee growing colder by the minute. Buck's mind was no where near home. During a night of restless sleep came a dream he had never had, true to his old dreams, Gunter was there, but not in the one where Buck held him as he died. Gunter had appeared in his dream, but he was sitting by a campfire, and he had a small dog beside him that he was feeding. He had just looked at Buck as if he were right beside him and said "Sleep in peace, for I have him in my arms", and then Gunter smiled.

Buck sat for a few more minutes, going over and over in his mind this dream that he had dreamed, when he heard a scratching at the door. Coming back to reality, Buck got up and walked to the door and let Turk inside.

"Well, I guess you're ready for some food, huh buddy!" said Buck

With a number of small growls and whining sounds, and a tail wagging furiously, Buck knew the answer.

Buck scooped a large bowl of food from the bag of dog food next to the refrigerator and poured it into Turks bowl and then dropped the measuring bowl back into the dog food bag. Turning back to see Turk just sitting by his bowl, first looking at his bowl of food, then looking back up at Buck, letting out just the slightest of whines.

"Now, you know Miss Gracie said you needed to cut out bacon, you are getting too fat" said Buck with little authority in his voice.

Turk just sat there, first cocking his head to the left and then the right, and again just the smallest of whines escaped Turks mouth.

"Oh, okay but you better not let Gracie know!" said Buck as he gave in one more time.

Walking to the cupboard with Turk in close pursuit, Buck reached in and pulled out a piece of beef jerky. Turk spotting his prize started going around in circles, and if dogs could talk, you would almost swear Turk was saying "Thank you, thank you, thank you."

Walking back to the table and picking up his cup of coffee, Buck looked up as he raised the cup to his lips, and out of the darkness he saw a light come on at Gracie's house.

"Thank God, she is finally awake" said Buck as he turned and poured the still half full cup of coffee into the sink. Looking at Turk who had just started eating from his dog bowl Buck said "You can stay here and finish, I will be back later."

Gracie was standing by the coffee maker with expectations of a cup of coffee when she heard a vehicle and then saw head lights pulling into her driveway.

"What in the world is he doing here this early!" said Gracie, as she glanced at the clock that read 4:15. Walking to the back door, Gracie had just turned the deadbolt to unlock the door when Buck reached the door. Gracie turned away from the door and proceeded to walk back to the coffee maker. Buck stood outside the door for just a second before realizing Gracie wasn't going to open it. Opening the door and walking in, Buck stopped in the open doorway and watched Gracie as she proceeded towards the other side of the kitchen.

"I guess I'm a little early, huh?" said Buck

Standing by the coffee maker watching the last few drops fall into the coffee pot, Gracie turned her head in Bucks direction and said "Just a tad bit, Bobby."

"I'm sorry, honey, it's just that I couldn't sleep and I have been waiting for a couple of hours for you to get up, and when I saw your light I couldn't wait to talk to you" said Buck.

Gracie poured herself some coffee and after taking a couple of sips walked over to the kitchen table and started to sit down.

"Well, come on in and shut the door, want some coffee?" asked Gracie

"Yeah, sure, but sit down, I can get it" said Buck

Buck poured himself a cup of coffee and, pulling a chair out opposite Gracie, sat down and looked across at her.

Gracie sat there for a few seconds looking at Buck and said "What...why are you just sitting there looking at me?"

"I was just waiting to see if you were ready to talk yet. I know you are not really a morning person. At least not until you have had at least one cup of coffee" answered Buck

"Okay...what is it you want to say that is so important?" asked Gracie

"I had another dream about Gunter last night...

"Baby, you know I'm sorry that you have those dreams, but...

"No, no this time it was different, this time it was a good dream. After all these years I can finally let go, I think" said Buck with a slight smile on his face.

"What happened?" asked Gracie with a quizzical look on her face.

"Well, I was tossing and turning most of the night, then I must have fallen into a deeper sleep, and I dreamed. In my dream I saw Gunter sitting by a campfire, still dressed in fatigues and he had his bush hat on. He was feeding this little puppy what looked like hot dogs, and he just looked at me and smiled. Then he said "Sleep in peace, for I have him in my arms" and then he was gone." said Buck

"Now, what do you think it means?" asked Gracie

"He was very calm, and peaceful…and I think he is happy." answered Buck

"And when he said "I have him in my arms" do you think he meant BJ?" asked Gracie.

"Yeah, I'm sure he meant BJ, I just don't know if he meant BJ's body or his spirit, that is why I had to come down here, I'm am getting really worried about BJ" answered Buck.

"If you don't mind a little woman's intuition, I feel that he is still okay…and I don't think he is too far away" said Gracie with a slight smile on her face.

"That's one of the things I love about you, Gracie, your positive attitude" said Buck.

"Love?" asked Gracie

"Well, yeah baby, I love a lot of things about you" said Buck

"Yeah, but you never say "you love me" said Gracie

"I just figured you knew that" explained Buck

"Buck, a person needs to be told that, even if they kind of know it. Too many people go through life thinking the other person knows they're loved. My father never told me he loved me. I know he did, but, I don't know how to explain it. If he would have just once said he loved me, it would have been more total." said Gracie as the tears welled up in her eyes.

Buck looked across the table at Gracie for a few seconds, and without saying a word, stood up and walked around the table and stood beside Gracie looking down at her. When Gracie looked up she was shocked to see not Buck, but the

Bobby she knew standing there. Gracie stood up and was enfolded in Bobby's arms, and he whispered in her ear "I love you now, I have loved you always, and I will love you forever and a day."

And Gracie wept.

After holding each other for a moment or so, the pair separated, and after a gentle kiss, sat back down at the table beside each other.

"I'm sorry I'm crying, it's just that I have waited so long to hear that from you, and I love you too!" said Gracie.

"But, baby, I told you just the other day that I loved you" said Buck

"Honey, we have been apart for over ten years, you have a lot of catching up to do" said Gracie as she leaned over and kissed him.

"Yeah, your right, I love you, I love you, I love you…"

"That's enough, smarty pants" said Gracie with a smile.

"So, what gets you up so early this morning anyway?" asked Buck

"Karen down at the Southside Cafe called me late last night, seems one of her girls got sick and she wanted to know if I would fill in for her today and I told her I would.

I have to be there by six" answered Gracie as she looked at the clock.

"In fact, I need to get ready, what are you going to do today?" asked Gracie

"I have some stuff to do around the place, fix up BJ's room for one" answered Buck.

"Well, I have to get ready, you going to wait while I do?" asked Gracie

"No, I'm going back home, I might drop into town for lunch later" answered Buck.

Gracie walked Buck to the door and kissed him goodbye.

"I do love you" said Buck.

"And I love you" said Gracie.

As Buck drove back towards his place, the first light of day was just starting to break in the east and Buck thought "This is going to be a good day."

Chapter Thirty-Seven

BJ rolled over on his left side and the light of the rising sun shone on his face causing him to squint. Rolling back over on his right side BJ opened his eyes. Lying there he surveyed what he could see. The campfire was smoldering with just the slightest trail of smoke rising from it. Just past the fire where the man had slept, BJ could see his sign laying and beyond that, past the edge of the bridge, BJ could see a light fog laying along the river's shore. Lying there for a moment or so, BJ remembered the puppy and sat straight up and started rapidly searching around for his dog. Looking down to his left, a big smile came across BJ's face as he spotted "Traveler."

"Come here, boy, come here" called BJ.

Traveler's head came up at the sound of B.J's voice and he scampered up the slope towards him.

BJ, seeing him running toward him, covered his head with the blanket just before Traveler got to him. The two wrestled around in the blanket for a few minutes, one laughing and the other growling.

"Okay, okay that's enough" said BJ as he stood up.

BJ stood there, and for the first time, noticed that the stranger from the night before was no where to be seen.

"Hum, guess he got up and left" said BJ looking at Traveler who just sat there cocking his head.

After BJ took care of business and rolled up his blanket, he walked down to the river and washed up the best he could. Walking back to his backpack BJ scooped up the puppy and tried to put him in the pack. After several attempts, and Traveler not cooperating, BJ said "Okay I guess your going to have to walk until you get tired enough to want to be carried."

Walking out from under the bridge and up onto the highway, BJ had to stop and look around at how beautiful this area was. The valley was really just a wide area of flat land with the hills on either side and the river running down this side of it. But it was the sunrise and the way the light hit the fog along the river that had BJ captivated. All BJ could think to say was "Thank you, God."

After standing there for a few moments taking this all in, BJ decided it was time once again to put one foot in front of the other. After looking back to the south, and seeing no vehicles coming, BJ and Traveler started walking north.

BJ could see a few lights on in the town up ahead, and as he got closer and with the sunlight growing brighter, he watched as these lights were turned off one at a time. "Well, hopefully Traveler, tonight we will be turning our own light off" said BJ with a sigh.

As the pair walked up to the combination gas station, cafe, and post office (the entire downtown of Milton), BJ reached inside his pocket to find only some change. Standing outside the front door of the cafe, BJ counted his change "Well, Traveler, looks like we might be eating a little light."

At that same time BJ heard a scuffle on the pavement behind him, and turning saw an old man in bib overalls bending over and picking something up off the ground right behind BJ.

"I think you dropped this, young fella" said the old man as he held out a five dollar bill.

"Oh no, Sir, that's not mine" said BJ.

"Nonsense, I saw it drop from your pocket" replied the old man as he shoved the bill towards BJ.

More out of reflex than anything else, BJ's hand reached out and the old man put the bill in his hand.

"Well, thank you, Sir" said BJ.

"No need to thank me, I try to do at least one good deed a day. When I get an opportunity to do one this early in the day, I just consider it a blessing" and with that said, the old man walked up to the front door and went inside the cafe.

BJ stood there for a second or two and then looking around, thought "Where did he come from?"

BJ walked inside the Cafe/Store and was immediately told "Ain't no dogs allowed in here, son!"

Looking up at the man behind the store counter BJ said "I don't have any way to keep him outside, and if I set him down outside he might run out in traffic and get run over."

The man reached down behind the counter and came up with a piece of rope and handing it to BJ said "Here you can tie him up outside."

Reaching for the rope, BJ said "Thank you, Sir."

After tying Traveler to a post and calming him as much as possible, BJ went back inside the store. He picked up some cinnamon rolls and milk for him, and after looking around the store, picked up some beef jerky for Traveler. Figuring he liked both, and was sure Traveler would too, he walked up to the counter.

The old man from out front was standing by the coffee machine putting a lid on his cup as BJ approached the counter, and BJ said "Thank you, again" and the old man just smiled and nodded his head.

"Will that be all you need" asked the man behind the counter.

"Yes, Sir, and a ride to Burwell" said BJ with a smile.

"Cute kid!" said the man with a scowl.

"I was just joking, sorry" said BJ.

The man behind the counter added up BJ's purchase and said "That will be $4.37, and I'm not joking."

BJ handed the clerk the five dollar bill and waited for his change as the old man came up to wait his turn to pay.

"Here's your change" said the clerk.

BJ took his change, and seeing a jar on the counter with a little girls picture on it, dropped the change in the jar and turned and walked out the front door.

The old man walked up across from the man behind the counter and said "That was a pretty nice thing that young man just did."

The man behind the counter said "You don't know the half of it, mister, that's my daughter on the jar."

The old man paid for his coffee with the correct change and said "No, Sir, you don't know the other half, that young man was out in front counting his change so he could buy his dog something to eat, and I pretended he dropped that five on the ground and gave it to him. That change he left you was basically all he had. I told him about doing someone a good deed would make his day. You ought to try it." With that, the old man walked to the door, stopped and turned, and said "Your daughter is going to be fine" then opened the door and left.

BJ and Traveler sat out in front of the store and had their breakfast. Having no bowl for traveler, BJ poured the milk into his palm and laughed as Traveler lapped the milk up.

Finishing their breakfast, BJ untied traveler and the pair proceeded north. After a mile or so, Traveler was starting to lag behind and even sat down a few times. BJ stopped and took off his pack and had no trouble getting Traveler inside. With Traveler up on his back, BJ found the going much easier.

Another mile or so the road started going up an incline as they had reached the other side of the valley and were proceeding into the hills once again. BJ was bracing himself for the climb when he heard the sound of an approaching vehicle. Turning and sticking out his thumb, BJ spotted a bright red pickup coming towards him. The pickup came to a stop right beside him, and inside was a man driving, and what was probably his teenage son sitting on the passenger side.

"You the young man headed to Burwell?" asked the man.

With a surprised look on his face, BJ replied "Well, yes Sir, but how did you know?" "My brother Chris owns the store you just stopped at. He called me and asked if I was going to cattle auction and if I would give you a ride." explained the man.

"I would sure appreciate it sir" said BJ.

"No, I appreciate what you did for my niece" said the man

BJ stood there for a second trying to decide where to ride then said "I'll just ride in the back with my dog."

"Wherever you want, by the way my name's Joe, and this is my son, Jonathan" said Joe "My friends call me BJ" said BJ.

"Nice to meet you, BJ" said Jonathan as he extended his hand and they shook.

"Well, climb on in and we'll get you to Burwell.

BJ sat in the back of the truck as it rolled along over hills and through the small towns. BJ felt a lot lighter knowing that his hitchhiking days were over, but another thought hung heavy on his mind "What if his uncle didn't want him", but he would cross that hurdle when he came to it. Right now he was grateful for the ride.

Passing through Broken Bow, the biggest town he had seen in Nebraska, BJ broke out the jerky he had bought and he and Traveler had started a bad habit for the dog. Traveler liked beef jerky.

Half an hour later they passed through Sargent and on through more hills. A short time later BJ felt the truck slowing, and turned towards the front of the truck and hollered "Is this Burwell?"

"No, this is Taylor, Burwell is the next town, about fifteen miles and you will be there." answered Joe

"All right, thank you" answered BJ.

BJ sat back down with his back to the cab and felt a rush of anxiety come over him. A mixture of happiness and fear. Happy to be getting there, and scared of what might happen. This could be the end of the line, or the beginning of a life on the road. BJ could feel the anxiety building as each mile passed.

The truck made a right turn off the highway and they were no longer heading north. They were headed east. Every now and then BJ could see a river that was running along side the road, and only then did he realize he was in another valley like this morning. BJ watched as farm houses were passed by and started wondering if he would live in one of these, or if his uncle lived in town. What if his uncle didn't even live here anymore. Oh my God!

"Okay, slow down" thought BJ to himself. But the anxiety was running rampant. Traveler was being petted at a rapid pace, but didn't seem to mind.

BJ figured they had to be getting close, so he turned where he could look out around the driver's side and saw four tall silos sticking up above a stand of trees off to his left, "We're getting close, Traveler" BJ said nervously.

"Where do you want dropped off, BJ" hollered Joe out the window.

Not sure how to answer, BJ just said "In town will be fine"

The truck rolled over a small hill and BJ could see across a corn field the four silos perfectly clear, and his heart skipped a beat.

The truck came up to a street between the corn fields and made a left turn. Now BJ could really see the town. The truck slowed to twenty miles an hour and BJ saw a sign that read "Welcome to Burwell" and he felt a huge lump grow in his throat, this was his Dad's town.

The truck rolled slowly down the street past two blocks of homes, then they were downtown. BJ watched as they passed a movie theater and a furniture store and they were at a stop sign. They were in downtown Burwell. The truck made a left and they passed stores on both sides, half a block up they made a right.

"You let me know where you want out, okay?" asked Joe

The truck went up halfway, and BJ saw a bar on the corner of a road heading west out of town, and then a grocery store, and then they were making another right turn. BJ saw a place called "Southside Cafe," and then a car dealership, and as they were turning right again halfway up this block, there was another road heading east out of town. Past the other half of this block they made another right, and were back at the movie theater.

"What do you say, BJ" asked Joe.

"This is fine, you can let me out here" answered BJ.

Joe pulled into an angle parking place, and both him and his son got out. BJ was just climbing out of the truck when Joe said "You have never been here before, have you, son?" "No, Sir, I'm here to find my uncle" answered BJ.

Joe looked over BJ's shoulder and said "Well we could go in there and get some help."

BJ turned and looked in the direction Joe was looking and seeing "Police Station" above the door looked backed at Joe and as calmly as he could, said "No thank you, I'll ask around, I'm sure someone knows him."

"Suit yourself, I'm kind of hungry what about you" asked Joe.

"Yeah, come on, we could ask about your uncle over at the restaurant around the corner" exclaimed Jonathan.

"I'm not really hungry, but that is a good place to ask" said BJ.

"Well, climb back in and we'll drive over there" said Joe

Joe drove back around the square and parked in the parking lot along the side of the "Southside Cafe."

"We can put your pup up in front while we are inside, might want him to go to the bathroom first, though" said Joe as he climbed out of his truck.

"Yeah, thanks. Can I leave my pack and stuff in the back?" asked BJ.

"Sure, we will go on inside and get a table while you take care of your dog" said Joe, as BJ was setting Traveler on the ground.

After about five minutes Traveler was ready to go in the truck. BJ left the driver's side window down a little and closed the door. Traveler was immediately up on the window and barking madly.

"You be good and maybe it won't be long before you won't have to be in any more trucks." said BJ.

Walking to the front of the Cafe and around the corner to the front door, BJ could hear Traveler howling.

BJ reached for the door knob and twisting it was instantly reminded of Cotton's place near Centerville. Opening the door BJ stepped up one step right into what was a combination restaurant and bar. The wooden floor showed years of traffic. Along the left side of the room was a bar with stools, and then the rest of the area was filled with tables. Tables also lined the wall on the right side. Some tables sat six, but most were made for four. Once BJ's eyes became accustomed to the light, he spotted Joe and Jonathan sitting by the wall. BJ walked over to the table and sat down on the same side as Jonathan on the outside chair.

The trio had been there less than a minute when the waitress walked up with two ice teas and sat them down in front of Joe and his son.

"Well, you finally made it in, what would you like to drink, honey?" asked Gracie"

"Ice tea would be fine, Maam" answered BJ.

"Okay, one tea it is, I'll be right back for your order" said Gracie

Joe looked over at BJ and said "This is on me"

"Oh no, you have done enough for me" exclaimed BJ.

Gracie walked back to the table and sat the tea by BJ and said "What will you guys have?"

"Hamburgers and fries sound good, guys?" asked Joe

With nods of approval from both boys, Gracie asked "All the way?"

With nods from all three, Gracie turned and said "They will be right up"

BJ turned and looked around the room. Turning back to Joe, he asked "Who do you think would be the best to ask?"

"I imagine the best person to ask would be the waitress, probably knows everyone" answered Joe

"Yeah, I'll ask her after we eat, and thanks again" said BJ.

The hamburgers came and BJ ate his long before the others were half way through theirs.

"I guess you were hungrier than you thought" said Joe with a smile.

"Yeah, and it was awful good, I don't remember ever having a hamburger that good" stated BJ.

"So how long you been hitchin?" asked Joe

"Lets see, Centerville, Pauls Valley, Salinas, Milton and today. I left Houston five days ago." answered BJ.

Gracie had just cleared a table near them and was passing by their table when Joe said "Houston, Texas?"

Everyone in the room jumped at the sound of crashing plates and glasses that were dropped as Gracie turned to look back at the trio by the wall.

"What about Houston?" asked Gracie, as the other waitress came over to help her. "This young man here just told me he hitchhiked from Houston" said Joe.

"BJ!" exclaimed Gracie, as she placed her finger tips to her lips.

"Yes, Maam" answered BJ with a quizzical look on his face.

"You're Bill's son?" asked Gracie with tears starting to run down her cheeks.

"Yes, Maam, Bill Stephens' son" answered BJ.

Gracie bent over and hugged BJ the best she could and kept repeating "Thank you God, Thank you God."

"Excuse me, excuse me" cried BJ.

Standing back up Gracie said "I'm sorry, I'm Gracie, Oh let me look at you. Are you alright?" asked Gracie

"Yeah, I'm fine, are you the Gracie from the pond?" asked BJ.

"You know about Gracie's Pond?" asked Gracie, while wiping tears away and smearing mascara.

"Yeah, Dad told me all about that day, it's good to meet you finally" said BJ.

"So you know my uncle, too, then?" asked BJ with a slight tremor in his voice.

"Know him…Oh yes I know him, and is he ever going to be glad to see you!" answered Gracie excitedly.

"Glad…did you say glad?" and the dam burst, all of BJ's fears were relinquished with that one word and he stood up and fell into Gracie's waiting arms, and let go all the tears he had been holding back.

"Oh yes, child, you just let it go" said Gracie

After a minute or so they separated and sat down with Joe and Jonathan. Sitting across from BJ, Gracie held both of his hands and then said "I can definitely see your father in you, I am so sorry for what happened."

"I have to excuse myself, where is the restroom?" asked BJ.

"Right back through that door, second door on the right" answered Gracie.

Gracie sat back in the chair and exhaled loudly "I'm sorry, we have just been so worried."

"So, what happened?" asked Joe

"His Dad was killed about a month ago, his Mom about a year and a half ago. As far as I can figure, he left Texas to stay out of the orphanages. Left last week and, believe or not, hitchhiked up here" answered Gracie.

"So, where do you guys come in?" asked Gracie

"BJ did something for my brother, just a little gift from his heart, and it has changed my brother almost immediately. I have a niece that needs an operation. I don't know how to explain it, really. All my brother kept saying is that his faith in God was restored. When I saw my brother's eyes this morning, I knew. Somehow my brother knows my niece is going to make it through. I brought BJ up from Milton, it's the least I could do. I have never been much of a believer in angels, but I don't know." answered Joe.

BJ came back to the table and sat down. Looking across at Gracie, he just smiled. "Well, big guy, we got to be going" said Joe as he stood up from the table.

The four of them walked up to the front of the Cafe by the register.

"When do you think I will see Uncle Bobby?" asked BJ.

"If I can get off, we can leave right away" answered Gracie.

"Well, these guys have got to go, and I have something in their truck that belongs to me. I'll go get it and you can ask, if that's alright?" asked BJ.

"Yeah, Yeah sure, you go ahead on" said Gracie

The three of them walked out into the parking lot, and as soon as they were spotted, the yipes filled the air. Traveler did not like being left alone.

"Looks like everything is going to work out" said Joe

"Yeah, looks like it. I want to thank you again" said BJ.

"If you're ever down in Milton, give me a shout, just stop in at the store, my uncle will get a hold of me. Hang in there okay?" said Jonathan

Opening the door brought great relief to the surrounding area, and BJ was covered in puppy kisses. BJ pulled his pack out of the back of Joe's truck and stood out of the way as the pair pulled out of the parking lot. They were all still waving as the truck went around the corner of the square and out of sight.

BJ was standing in the small parking lot trying to figure what to do with Traveler when he saw Gracie come around the corner of the building.

"Well, what have we got here?" asked Gracie with a smile.

"Traveler, meet Gracie" said BJ introducing them.

"Well hello, Traveler, I guess you have lived up to your name" said Gracie.

"What are we doing?" asked BJ.

"Well, we are fixing to take you home, how about it?" asked Gracie

"Is it very far from here?" asked BJ.

"Seven and a half miles exactly, put your stuff in the truck" said Gracie.

"Wow, you drive a truck?" asked BJ.

"Doesn't everybody?" answered Gracie, and they both laughed.

"I guess I'll ride in the back with Traveler" said BJ.

"Nonsense, dogs are required to ride in the front, if they ride with me" said Gracie.

Pulling out of town BJ realized they were going the same way that he had come into Burwell as they passed the silos and turned back down the same highway.

"I think this is the way we came in" said BJ.

"Oh it is, Joe said he was from Milton, and this is the way you go to Milton" said Gracie. "I guess I was lucky they were going to the auction here today" said BJ.

"Well, honey, there wasn't any auction today" stated Gracie.

BJ just turned and looked out the window and silently said "Thank you God."

Gracie turned off the highway onto a gravel road, and BJ was immediately reminded of the man with the daughters as he watched the dust blow up behind the truck. Gracie drove by her place and she said "That's my place right there, and your place is straight up there," pointing towards the house a half a mile ahead.

"Is Uncle Bobby up here?" asked BJ.

"He is supposed to be working on some things around here, getting ready for you" Gracie answered.

The truck pulled up to the gate and BJ saw the sign with the two "B"s sitting on the rocker, and then looked at Gracie.

"We got the "Rockin Bs" back again, it's been too long" said Gracie, her voice trailing off as she ended.

Pulling through the gate across the cattle guard, BJ was taking it all in. Looking to his left he saw the pond he had heard so much about, and he could feel his throat closing as a too familiar lump started to grow, and then from around the back of the house came a black dash on three legs.

"What is that?" asked BJ.

"That's a Turk, your Uncle's prize possession!" answered Gracie

"He only has three legs!" said BJ excitedly.

"He actually has four, you will see when he turns toward us" said Gracie.

Turk met up with the truck and picked up the scent of Traveler immediately, and started raising cane.

"Is it going to be alright?" asked BJ.

"Oh yes, Turk is a big baby, he just smells your dog" said Gracie.

As the truck pulled up by the front steps with Turk in close pursuit, Gracie heard Buck hollering "I'm back here, honey!"

Gracie turned off the truck and hollered at Turk to get down as she opened her door. BJ made no motion to get out and held on to Traveler with all his might, as Traveler wanted to meet Turk.

"BJ, it's okay, look at this big baby" said Gracie.

Looking out the window at Turk who was patiently waiting for them to get out, his tail wagging furiously, BJ opened the door and the two dogs were together in a heart beat.

"See, it's okay, dogs instinctively know when they are puppies" said Gracie.

BJ looked at the dogs and Traveler had squatted and Turk was licking the top of Traveler's head as if cleaning him.

"Now you stay right here and I'll go get your uncle" said Gracie."

"Okay, I'll watch the dogs" said BJ, as he was being checked out by Turk.

Gracie was just about around the corner of the house when she heard Buck holler again. "I'm coming" said Gracie, as she passed from BJ's view around the back of the house. When she saw what Buck was doing, she stared in disbelief, Buck, looking over and seeing her staring, said "What?"

"You are really going all out for BJ, aren't you. These windows haven't been washed in over a decade" said Gracie, barely able to contain herself.

"I want him to see what someday will be his" said Buck.

"Well, it wont be long" said Gracie.

"What won't be long?" asked Buck.

"Before he will be looking out them...he's in the front yard" said Gracie, as tears of joy started cascading down her cheeks.

"He's here..."

"Yes"

"Right out front?"

"Yes"

Buck took a couple of steps towards the corner of the house then stopped and turned back to Gracie, "You are coming with me, aren't you, I mean what do I say?" "I will be right behind you, and speak with your heart" said Gracie.

BJ was bent over petting Turk when he felt someone looking at him. BJ straightened up and turned towards the corner of the house, and there he saw a replica of his father.

Buck stood there for a second himself as he felt his throat constrict, for before him stood his brother of long ago. Buck could feel the tears starting to run down his cheeks, and he felt no shame as he heard Gracie say "Go to him."

Buck stood as tall as he could, wiped the tears from his cheeks, and walked to BJ. BJ stood as tall as he could, wiped the tears from his face, and took the few steps it took for the two of them to be within handshake distance.

"Well, young man, I see you made it" said Buck.

"Yes, Sir, was quite a trip" said BJ.

"You remind me so much of your father when he was a boy" said Buck a little less gruffly.

BJ started to speak, but his voice broke, so he stopped.

BJ started again "You remind me so much of my father."

BJ stood there looking at Buck and his lips began to quiver, and tears began to fall down his cheeks.

Buck stood there and in his mind he heard "Speak with your heart."

Buck took a step forward, opened his arms and pulled BJ to his chest and held him as he cried.

"I'm Glad you made it home" said Buck, as a tear fell on BJ's shoulder.

About the Author

Fighting for his life from the day he was born prematurely in a small town in Indiana. The author was to find his life anything but boring.

Moving to another small town in central Florida the author found fishing and camping in the swamps one of his greatest pleasures and to this day is still an avid fisherman.

As a teenager he liked hunting. But after two tours to Vietnam the author had all the hunting he could handle. Going into thick woods or swamps with a gun is more than he can handle.

After many heartbreaking relationships he found himself in a 12 Step Program in 1982. He found out he was not alone or the square peg in a round hole, never fitting in.

Today after 16 years of recovery he is married to his best friend, Christine. His wife of 13 years. Together they have five children and four grandchildren. Life is good.

The author hopes that the solutions to loss, grief and despair found by him will help others find the light at the end of the tunnel.

Today he lives in the country forty three miles northwest of Houston, Texas. He is living life one day at a time.